## PRAISE FOR GINA KINCADE

"Gina Kincade is imaginative, intelligent, and full of heart. It really takes a special writer to not only craft attention-grabbing, complex plots, but to also write three-dimensional characters that come alive on the page and in your hearts."
— Amazon Reviewer, TOP 100 REVIEWER

"A Shot at Love by Gina Kincade, was a very well done, emotionally moving story of an eagle shifter in love with a panther shifter. These two men were very attractive characters in different ways, and I loved how they were together. I hadn't read anything by Gina Kincade before and I loved her writing style."
— *Amazon Customer*

I devoured this story in one sitting and could have easily read an entire series of just these characters, this world, and this story. It really takes a special write to not only craft such an attention-grabbing plot, but to also write three-dimensional character that come alive on the page and in your hearts. This is a story I will not soon forget, and the emotions I felt while reading will surely haunt my thoughts for days to come."

— Amazon Reviewer, TOP 100 REVIEWER

OMG!! Hot, Hot Hot!!!!

"A very short story about Micah and Jason finding love! I sooo needed more of these two! The chemistry and the emotions between them were amazing!!!! Hope to get to see more of these two!"

— *Amazon Customer*

Cowboy hats off to Gina Kincade & Kiki Howell, who are both so phenomenally talented!! Combine their talents with their natural gifts for crafting impossible to put down stories, and Voila! Their Author Magic transforms this from being "just a story" into one helluva sweet & spicy/hot cowboy romance adventure worth living over & over again!

— Cherri-Anne Boitson, Leather & Lace Reviews Voted 2nd Favorite Book Reviewer of 2015

"What a fantastic story. Sexy, erotic and a great story. What a combination. The only problem? I wanted more!!! Can't wait to read more of Gina's work!"

— *John Miller*

What Lies Within Us by Kiki Howell & Gina
Kincade
"Beauty stole her already shallow breath." Can't
tell you how truly magical that sounds.
—While that is an abbreviated quote/line from
the story, it so aptly summed up my reaction &
feelings to this story!
The detailed descriptions of everything from the
storm to the magical objects and spells brings this
whole new dynamic to the story, enriching it,
adding depth, bringing to life every single part of
the story, no matter how big, small or even how
inconsequential it *may* seem. It truly is What
Lies Within Us that makes this story the magical
gem that it is!
— Cherri-Anne Boitson, Leather & Lace Reviews
Voted 2nd Favorite Book Reviewer of 2015
Top 1% Reviewer on Goodreads

"Great storyline with characters that make the pages steam. Loved all the Christmas elements added into this spicy little tale. Do yourself a favor and gift yourself this story then, then put yourself on the naughty list by taking some time to indulge in this read."

— *Kirstein Howell, Vine Voice*

"Having just spent the afternoon reading this wonderful book, I have to say that not only it is as captivating as it is sexy. The story moves along at a fast and furious pace taking you into a world of whirlwind romance and the paranormal. It kept me on the edge of my seat taking me into the story with every page."

— *Amazon Customer*

This was a really fun, and hot, read. I spent most of the story grinning, heart pounding, eager for what would happen next. It's so great to see Gina writing again, as we're gifted with gems like On Santa's Naughty List. This story made me wish that I was in an area where we got a White Christmas, because it's perfect to warm you up on a cold winter's day.

Regardless of the temperature of the day, this is a scorching read. It aims to delight, and succeeds. I highly recommend it for anyone after some Christmas kink!

*— Casey Kerwitz, Amazon Reviewer*

When the Snow Flies: Shifter Paranormal Romance

*Out of Print*
Alpha Shifters Seductions Boxed Set
Alphas On The Prowl Boxed Set

*Other Edited Titles Still Available*
The Wolf In The Neighborhood: Werewolf Shifter Paranormal Romance (The Wolf Smitten Book 1)
Once Bitten, Twice Shy: Werewolf Shifter Paranormal Romance (The Wolf Smitten Book 2)
Leader of the Pack: Werewolf Shifter Paranormal Romance (The Wolf Smitten Book 3)
Wolf Smitten Full Series Boxed Set: Werewolf Shifter Paranormal Romance (The Wolf Smitten Books 1-3)

"Kiki Howell spins a wonderful tale of passion, magic, betrayal, and a love that conquers all."
— NY Times Bestselling Author, Hannah Howell about Torn Asunder

"I think this is the most romantic novel I've ever read! True love cannot and should not be stopped because of physical differences between two people."
— 5 Howls by Emi at Bitten by Paranormal Romance about A War in the Willows Trilogy

"Ms. Howell's novella…sang to me. It will to you too."
— Justine, *eBook Addict Reviews* about The Sorcerer's Songs

"Kiki's use of words and descriptions is indescribable and weaves a kind of magic around the reader."
— Melissa, *ParaNormal Romance Reviews* about The Healing Spell

The Magic was in the Chocolate

The Healing Spell

The Witch's Beast

Working out the Kinks

Sacred Sex

Snowed In

When the Snow Flies: Shifter Paranormal
Romance

Beyond the Veil: Paranormal & Magical
Romance Boxed Set

Under the Veil: Paranormal & Magical Romance
Short Story Boxed Set

Alpha Heat: 21 Tantalizing Contemporary &
Paranormal Romance Short Stories Boxed Set

Alpha Shifters After Dark (Shifter Paranormal
Romance Boxed Set)

Put Your Ho Ho's On Holiday Boxed Set

Cowboy Boots and Handcuffs

Majors Creek Ranch Series Book One

A Contemporary Western Erotic Romance

Published by Naughty Nights Press LLC

http://naughtynightspress.com/

First Individual Print Edition July 2016

First Individual Digital Edition July 2016

ISBN: 978-1-926514-39-0,

978-1-926514-38-3

Originally Published in Print & Ebook in the

Alpha Fever: Paranormal & Contemporary

Romance Boxed Set

March 2016

ISBN: 978-1-926514-30-7,

978-1-926514-34-5,

978-1-926514-37-6

# Cowboy Boots and Handcuffs

## Majors Creek Ranch

### Book One

## CHAPTER ONE

Kathryn looked around at her newest prison cell, another small, barely-decorated bedroom in yet another guy's, or should she say guard or warden's place. This time the condo of one Jake or Jason something or other. He had taste similar to a saltine cracker; nothing in the condo except some cream-like paint on the walls and a few pieces of well-worn furniture. She couldn't believe anyone actually lived here. Her room at boarding school had looked better than this, even before she'd hired a decorator to make it livable.

With an audible sigh, she moved her ear to hover close to where the door to her room sat cracked back open, after having slammed it shut for effect. She quieted her angry thoughts, wanting to hear the conversation going on about ten steps away in the living room. This place was so ridiculously tiny, even with separate bedrooms–a thin excuse for a wall between them–for all intents and purposes they would have to be considered sleeping together. Regardless of close proximity, the guy who had brought her here talked loudly, even in response to the new guy's obvious whispering in a tight voice, clearly displaying his hints at attempting to keep their voices down. Derrick, however, the bodyguard she'd been staying with this past week–well five days, so close to a week–had already told her on their way over to the condo he was happy to be given the chance to wash his hands of her. Apparently dealing with her spoiled ass wasn't worth the hefty pay her father had promised him. Not really. So, the fact her stalker had once again found her had been a nice excuse for Derrick to pass her on to the next poor guard on the list.

"Spoiled," she said out loud to no one, restating the word Derrick had just used again, for like the hundredth time.

I'm not spoiled, just deserving. Daddy says so. I'm entitled to more than living like a prisoner in these low-class places with heathen–all muscles with no brains or class–guys watching my every move, loving looking down on me out of sheer jealousy. The words rumbled around in her brain so violently they were causing a headache. Or, maybe she was just hungry. Lord only knew what crap she'd be fed next. Even boarding school served better food than her wardens. Plus, when she demanded better, a five star restaurant with actual edible food, these guys acted so put out when it was their job to guard her wherever she wanted to go. Daddy had provided a food allowance, and her life wasn't supposed to change. He expected her to eat better, and she had said so when they tried to pass off sub-par meals like pizza in a box. Not that it hadn't tasted good, she had to admit, only if to herself, but that was not the types of foods she was accustomed to, or meant to eat. Like her father, the girls at school had confirmed her station in life, what she deserved, in the conversations she'd overheard at tables of those forced to sit around her. She had demanded her due as she'd been taught to do, like her father had commanded she be kept safe. These jerks were paid to serve and protect. Literally. At least Derrick had managed that in her short stay with him, the serve and protect thing, anyway. Conversations with him were nothing more than disinterested grunts in reply to anything she said along with a steady stream of eye rolls. He really needed a lesson in who was better than whom!

"Bet Miss I Deserve Better will drive you insane faster than she did me," Derrick said, a tight laugh accompanying his deep, anger-laced voice.

"We will be fine," Jason whispered back. He chuckled. "I'm surprised at you, Derrick, letting a young woman get the better of you, or at the very least under your skin like this."

"She didn't. She's being moved 'cause the stalker has found her again, not my inability to do the job. Guy's a real pro. Seems to be nowhere we can hide her he can't sniff her out. Regardless of the reason, you will soon be given the privilege of understanding what she's like. Not that I can't handle it, but no amount of money is worth handling some boarding school bi—. Sorry, boarding school princess for long. Miss high and mighty in there is a headache no one deserves. There's no such thing as conversation with her, just a self-boosting of her ego, 'hey, look how great I am,' or a barking of orders. The stalker did me a favor finding her. I get paid to protect, as I did, even serve, letting her lead as close to a normal life as possible while under my care. However, I don't get paid to play butler and errand boy to a demanding chick who thinks herself better than the entire population. Daddy should have hired her someone else for that and I could have protected that poor louse, too. Honestly, I don't even understand how a person gets to be like her. What happens in a girl's life to make them think like that? To be so brainwashed?"

"No, I can see she didn't get under your skin at all," Jason said, his voice sarcastically tight, his laugh escaping despite his attempt at control. "From what I read, Kathryn Caruthers is a motherless girl, raised in boarding schools due to her Senator father being re-married to politics, living between Sacramento and DC. She's had no one to teach her how to act other than other spoiled rich girls and boarding school employees paid well to cater to her every whim."

"Yeah, make excuses for her now, man," Derrick countered, his tone gaining the depth of defensiveness. "I'll talk to you in a day or two and see if you're still defending her."

"Come on, you have to start off by feeling sorry for her and go from there, finding your understanding—"

"Give it a rest. I'm done. Have a good time. It's almost time for her highness to be fed," Derrick spat out before she heard the front door slam.

"Sorry for me?" Kathryn hissed as she quietly closed her door, trapping herself in her new bedroom. She was stunned, having no way to mentally process such a thing as someone feeling sorry for her. She'd never known the concept before. Hate she knew, understood it happened out of jealousy. The pettiness of girls who excluded her at school, she got that, too. Jealousy. Simple. She was better than those other rich girls. They wanted all she had. Money and privilege bread loneliness, even for those who lived in privilege. It was the price she had to pay for being born to such a man as Senator Caruthers who had kept his seat in the house longer than she could remember. Any so-called friendship at school hadn't been real anyway. They'd chosen to associate with others who could make them look better. She had no need for that, having to watch every word you said lest someone get petty and spill all of your secrets out of spite.

She had no real memories of her mother, but people always said she got her beauty from her. What else could people say? Some girls were born models, blond hair, skinny bodies. She, on the other hand, had been born with a full face and curvy figure, but money could make anyone beautiful. The right hairdresser, the proper stylist could make anyone look what people could feel free to term beautiful if they felt they had to. Money, and all it could buy, was indeed gorgeous in its own way. Since she'd been brought to political functions as a young woman, or made to attend mixers at school, realized she'd realized she would never be anything more than a pity fuck, or a girl a man dated in a bid to get to her father. Her only goal was to find a guy from the pool of those deemed appropriate suitors who she could tolerate enough to marry.

She'd never get a guy based just on her looks, or have the luxury of waiting to fall in love. No, she would have to be married off long before that. But, she was fine with that. Marriages of convenience were more prevalent than anyone liked to admit in her world. To hear the girls at school go on about their parents was proof enough. Sometimes she wished she had a mother to ask things of, about all the crap that rolled off the tongues of the girls at school. Yet, she didn't, and she'd turned out just fine. Well, until the past few weeks, trapped with these goons paid to protect her. They'd taken her to whatever hairdresser they found, the one closest to wherever they'd had her shacked up, not the most reputable. Her long, mahogany locks were starting to show it. She fingered a big curl, less tamed than usual, and grimaced at the mirror on the back of the door, feeling sorry for herself. This was outrageous.

She formed a plan to march out there, demand to be taken shopping, to have her hair, and her nails done properly, and then be fed an appropriately edible meal. He felt sorry for her, so maybe this one would work out, attend to her needs as he should. The grin she flashed the mirror should have made her feel better. It didn't. Instead, with some odd sensation growing in the pit of her stomach, she let her hefty body fall to the sorry excuse for a bed, wincing as the springs loudly protested.

She let the brief image she'd gathered upon meeting Jason form in her brain. Solid. Tough. As they all were. Yet, she'd wanted to run her hand over the scruff on his face. She let herself off the hook for that one, deeming it some sort of curiosity with all the clean-cut type she normally met, dressed to the nines in high-priced suits. Jason's warm brown eyes had literally twinkled when he'd smiled at her, as if the man, any man for that matter, could be genuinely happy to see her. The small, dark curl of his hair around his ear, on his neck, had looked soft, inviting to touch, leaving her breathless and dumbfounded prior to being shown quickly to her room so Derrick could complain about her. The desires had disappeared quickly when she'd heard Derrick's voice, but now knowing she was alone in a small condo with the maybe nice guy, who felt sorry for her, something akin to lust laced in irritation rolled through her tightly held core. Becoming suddenly conscious of resting her hand on the soft pouch of her stomach, she couldn't help but wonder how hard Jason's abs must be.

She didn't even realize the thought of teasing her hand across his firm stomach brought a slight quirk to her full lips as smile spread across her mouth.

CHAPTER TWO

Jason Majors decided this was the most unusual case he'd ever had in his protective services career. A full time rancher and a part-time bodyguard for his best friend's firm, Jason knew his job and did it well, every single time. Up until now, that is.

Sure, he had watched out for and cared for some pretty big names in this business, but this one stood out beyond anyone he'd been assigned to prior.

Sequestered in a private school for more than

half her life, young Miss Caruthers was nothing more than an ordinary rich man's kid, really, but her Daddy was an honest man–a rarity in the political world–and he'd apparently pissed off the wrong people because of it. Sadly, honest or not, he'd raised a monster. One had to feel sorry for the guy, though. Surely he felt the need to make up for her not having a mother the only way he had the time and means to, by giving her everything he could, buying her stuff. Boarding school raised her.

To make the case for his assumptions, Kathryn presented as a typical little rich girl: Daddy's materialistic, spoiled brat used to getting everything she wanted. So, basically this case should have been simple with the ordinary, run-of the mill stalker out to payback the Senator for refusing a bribe, right? Wrong, it had been anything but ordinary. He'd catered to her every demand so far, these first days with her, honestly feeling sorry for her. He didn't believe she had a true friend in the world, and she definitely didn't have family in any real sense of the word. He figured he was being paid enough to take care of her in the manner she was accustomed to, or at least some semblance of it that he could pull off. What else did he have to do? It was his job to just stick by her, watch her, protect her as she lived her life as normally as she could under 'house arrest,' as she'd called it. He'd done his best to do his work. He just wished being around her wasn't such a physical hardship. Regardless of her attitude issues, a personality that needed some work through no real fault of her own, that body of hers... Well, there was a specific kind of suffering being around a woman who resembled a goddess in his eyes. Kathryn had every physical attribute he craved the way a pregnant woman craved food so bad it became a need.

"Stop it!" he chided himself, slamming his hand holding the remote down onto the couch, clutching the plastic control with a force that made his fingers ache. If his grip were any harder he'd crumble the stupid thing.

Bored with the random flicking through the channels—he wasn't paying attention to the images on the screen anyway–he pressed the power button and stared as the screen went dark. Standing with a stretch to rouse his tightened muscles, he sauntered into the kitchenette, and grabbing a bottle of water from the refrigerator, slipped out the sliding glass door, careful to leave it open just a crack behind him.

It was so unseasonably warm for early June here in California this year; he was starting to sweat already. Taking a long, slow swig from the bottle, he sighed audibly, lit a cigarette, and leaned against the wall. Filthy habit, smoking, he knew, but one he only indulged in on rare occasions and likely out of sheer boredom.

His attentive nature automatically alerted him to the man standing in the parking lot of the condo looking under the hood of his car and shaking his head. Somewhat suspicious, really, since the guy hadn't touched a thing yet. Jason watched him for a minute, mentally committing the guy's attributes to memory as he pulled smoke down deep into his lungs. Overhearing a one-sided conversation, assuming was the dude requesting a tow truck, his gut instinct determined the guy no true threat, and his gaze traveled on. The old lady walking her dog down the block did not even catch more than a glance. Scanning the entire visually accessible area in no time flat, he decided all was secure, figuring perhaps it was just too damn hot for many people to bother coming out tonight, even a stalker.

This was the fourth place they had taken the young lady, and he was the third man on the job; their best this time, according to Pete. His friend's last chance, really. It was getting to be too much, the pressure of this high profile client. Both he and Pete were worried they had a leak on the inside. The damn jerk always managed to find her, slipping notes under the door of her location no matter where they were, getting bolder each time. Besides her locations being compromised, the other two guys who'd had this job before him couldn't handle her anyway, and he'd started to understand why.

Drawing deep on his cigarette once again, he held the tainted breath for a moment and then exhaled loudly, the smoke getting caught in front of him in the still slightly muggy night air. From the corner of his eye he glimpsed a faint light on in Kathryn's bedroom through a part in the curtains. Damn woman! He'd told her to shut them tight. She presented a challenge in more ways than one. Definitely more, many more, ways than any other client he'd ever taken on.

Leaning slightly to the left, he realized he could see straight into her room where she lay on the bed, covered only by a thin sheet, the outline of her curvaceous body revealed as clear as if the sheet did not exist. His gaze followed the curve of the rounded nature of her breasts until he found himself perusing along her waist, then up over the small rise of her mound. He forced his stare to trace over the outline of her hips, more than generous for a man to grab hold of and...

Another deep drag of the cigarette helped him semi-refocus his wayward thoughts. Holding the smoke in, shutting his eyes tight, he willed away the glimmer of a desire to spank her for leaving the curtains open, reminding himself this young woman was his charge, not his consenting, willing partner. The dominant in him had taken quite the blow to his ego dealing with this woman these past few days. Shit, how he wanted to tame her, train her to obey his commands, to keep her safe despite the post's necessity.

Damn, something about this woman attracted him to her, and it seriously mucked with his professionalism in a huge way. Some kind of sizzling energy seemed to spasm in his gut any time she came into his immediate vicinity. Even now, as she lie sleeping, he had this uncanny weird feeling rushing through his veins and making his heart thud in his chest. He didn't get it. Not one of his charges before her had ever had this kind of effect on him. None of the women he'd know in his life had, for that matter. So why did his libido go into overdrive in response to this particular full-figured vixen with her soft looking, light mahogany curls trailing across the pillow? He was losing his edge over a spoiled little rich girl, for Christ sake! Apparently to his baser desires, when faced with such a voluptuous body, her attitude became a non-issue. It made no sense. He'd told himself quite a few times the poor girl was just a product of her upbringing, that the depth of a good woman just laid in wait under all of the privileged nonsense. Still, he couldn't justify the thought process or time he'd spent on it given she was literally a charge, a non-touchable mission to serve and protect. Of course, she gave new meaning to the word serve, and he'd no idea why he'd been waiting on her hand and foot to some degree. Wasn't like he was getting laid for his efforts. The idea of disciplining her grew as a more appealing idea daily.

Knowing it wrong, and he could get himself fired for it, he moved closer to the window as she rolled toward him in her sleep. The sheet had slipped down when she'd turned onto her side, revealing the most perfect set of pale, supple globes he had ever seen. Natural, too, which in this day and age was a rarity. She's been over-endowed by the gods, though, and his mouth watered with the thoughts of suckling on the rich flesh.

He just stood there, marveling at the way the diffused light from the bedside table only enhanced his view. His mind began to fill with thoughts, images of things he definitely shouldn't be envisioning.

He twisted away from the tantalizing image between the parted curtains, not even realizing he'd formed his left hand into a tight fist. Not before noticing she had her window open just a little as well, however. Holy Christ! Does this woman ever do what she is told? The imprint of his wide hand outlined in red on her ass came to mind, and he suddenly flexed his clenched hand, his fingers spread as if to spank the delectable large mounds.

Grinding out his cigarette with the toe of his pointed cowboy boot, he opened the sliding door and moved to go back inside when he heard a noise that sounded almost like an animal in pain. Moving quickly across the short span to her bedroom door, he called, "Kathryn, is everything okay?" Silence greeted him in response.

He shrugged, figuring it must have been a cat in heat outside her window or the like. She did have the damned thing open. He should go in and close it for her, but he didn't actually trust himself to walk through the room with her in such a state of undress. He'd be more than justified in doing so, of course, but the risks remained too great that no matter how it played out he would get fired. He couldn't risk that. Nothing posed a threat outside. He'd just made sure of it. More than wide awake, vigilantly attentive, he'd hear any changes.

Leaving the sliding glass door open to catch the light breeze that had drawn up, but closing the screen door to keep the bugs out, he strolled back to the living room and flopped back down on the couch with an audible sigh. Turning on the television, he lowered the volume until he could barely hear it, and began to aimlessly channel surf again. How he hated the night shift; sometimes it could be so damn long. Pictures flashed before him, meaningless, too fast to even discern what they were. Not that it mattered.

Within moments the strangled sound rang out again. Jabbing the mute button, he immediately cut the sound to the television completely. Jason rolled up off the afghan-covered old furniture and trotted back to the sliding door. Damn it, he couldn't see shit through the screen. Pushing the feeble visual obstruction to the side with a finger, he stepped out onto the brick-covered patio, slamming the flimsy, mesh-covered aluminum behind him.

Scanning the area once more, his steely gaze came to rest on the barest movement in a thatch of thick, shadowy green bushes about ten feet away. Glancing back at the entranceway to the condo and the curtain parted beside it, he crept over to the bushes, moving cautiously and quieter as he got closer. He launched himself at the shrubbery just as two cats darted out from beneath the boughs. He landed, hard, grabbing nothing but air.

"Shit!" Getting up and dusting himself off, he glanced around at the empty premises, thankful no one appeared to have witnessed his stupidity.

Strolling back to the open door of the unit at a hurried pace, although he hated to prove Derrick right, he contemplated again about leaving this job. Some of the shit things he had to do just didn't seem worth the blow to his ego anymore. Besides, he'd been working for Pete for over a decade now, and he'd been seriously considering just focusing his efforts on the ranch before this job even came up. Sighing, he promised himself he'd give it one more week, his best shot, for his friendship, and because he knew Pete really needed him on this right now. The Senator was too big a client for Pete to lose, and Jason was the best man for the job. He just seriously hoped it didn't take that long to catch this jackass running about the streets causing havoc for the Senator and his daughter, not to mention all the guys at the agency.

Just as he moved to go back into the condo, the sound, more like a moan now, drifted to his ears again, but this time he heard it clearly coming through the open window of the bedroom. He hesitated for a moment, not really wanting to go looking in on her while she slept. If he didn't look, though, she could be in some danger. It was his ass on the line as well as her life. Worst case, he might see that voluptuous body again, with those absolutely perfect boobs with their pink, ripe nipples. Groaning inwardly, he peeked through the window, observing her still on the bed, the sheet completely off this time. She couldn't have looked more ideal, her body more inviting than she did; right down to her perfectly manicured patch of hair between her thighs. She was alone, thankfully, on all accounts. Ironically, with his thoughts constantly derailing to devouring her well cared for human form, hearing her scream his name as he plunged deep into the heated apex between her thick thighs, he stood as the only true threat to her at this moment.

Just about to move away by sheer force of will, he detected something new in the vocal harmony emanating from her throat. Her guttural moans seemed to be akin to some sort of pleasure, apparently, despite the fact she remained alone. Obviously enjoying a nice dream. I can only guess what it's about.

He knew he should walk away, now, before he got himself in too deep. He shouldn't continue to gaze upon her with the physical reaction she had on him. Nothing actually threatened her. He didn't have to save her from her dreams, or even nightmares. Regardless, he stood outside the window and stared like a perverted stalker. Oh dear lord, her long, dark auburn-streaked curls spread out on the pillow around her, that curvaceous body, and those long legs with the artfully painted crimson toes were near about killing him. Damn, he could imagine her solid thighs wrapped tight around his hips as he thrust into her heat. The mental combination stopped him. She was simply so damn distracting, so delicious, so...fucking perfect. He'd always found women with more meat on their bones to turn his crank a hell of a lot more than the skin-on-a-stick type. Skinny wasn't his thing. Well, if it weren't for her prissy little rich bitch attitude, and the fact he was on a job he was supposed to be focusing on, she'd be a perfect match for the type of woman he preferred.

Feeling a painful thickness begin to develop behind his zipper at her continued pleasurable sounds, knowing in his gut she must truly be enjoying something pretty heavy in her dreams, he moved just an inch to make himself a little more comfortable, leaning heavily against the wall. He watched, enraptured as she slid her hand from where she'd been fondling her breast to down between her creamy thighs, dipping into the crevice and back out, repeatedly, and ever so gently.

Oh shit, now he was well and truly hooked. This up close and almost personal show stimulated more than anything he'd perused over the Internet when his libido got the better of him and release was a necessity. He wasn't a porn addict or anything, not by a long shot, but he definitely admitted to enjoying the scenes created with the intent to help him along the way to self-satisfaction when necessary. He was human, after all.

He hated himself at the moment, though. Self-loathing and raging hormones battled within. Even as his conscience told him to step the fuck away from that window, right now, his traitorous body encouraged him to stay put. As much as he knew this was wrong, he was taking advantage of his charge's innocence which made him feel much like a dirty old man, he could not move away even if he wanted to–which, truth be told, he didn't want to at all. The universe evidently decided to justify his continued appreciation of this beautiful woman. Kathryn definitely no longer dreamed, and evidently decided to continue the gratifying activity that had begun in her dream.

As Jason watched, like the stalker he'd sworn to protect her from, she opened her legs to allow easier access. He had a perfect view of those pink, glistening lips as she continued to rub her clit with one perfectly manicured thumb. He groaned as two of her red-tipped fingers dipped lower and finally pushed into her glorious, slick pussy. Holy Christ, this was enough to make a man mad! Creeping her like this, he felt more like a 'Peeping Tom' then a bodyguard! This was so not in his employment description, but here he was.

Her fevered pitch had increased to quite a loud level he began to wonder if the neighbors would hear her. Knowing he'd lose his job, probably ending his career entirely and losing his best friend in the process if he were caught, he still could not tear himself away from the damn window and the extremely stimulating scene happening just on the other side of those curtains! He knew in his gut he was very close to embarrassing himself. Not to mention he had a lot to lose here. Oddly, none of it seemed to matter in the face of seeing her like this. Fragile, all the hoity-toity, holier-than-thou attitude had disappeared and in its place remained a woman so full of passion it intrigued him all the more.

She began to move her digit faster over her clit, dipping the other two in and out of her glazed core. Over and over she pressed inside herself, then added a third, stretching her pink, moistened labia wide, nearly driving him over the brink as he panted like a dog in heat outside the window. Kathryn pumped her hand into her heat, keening with what he assumed an elusive release. Getting so obviously frustrated, she pumped, rubbed, and flicked the swollen bud with the rounded tip of her fingernail. She thrashed her head side to side on the bed. With a deep growl slipping from her lips, she reached into the drawer beside the bed and produced a silver, bullet shaped vibrator. Turning the speed on a loud, rumbling high he heard clearly through the small opening in the window, she touched the buzzing phallus to the very tip of her swollen clit, jumping a little when it connected. Another very audible moan bubbled up from her throat, and Jason's jeans suddenly felt extremely constrictive.

Rubbing the sliver shaft over her clit a few times, dipping it into her wet channel, presumably to help it glide, she began to pant heavily as her orgasm drew nearer. He watched as that little silver bullet flew over her clit.

Undoing two of the buttons on his jeans to

relieve some of the pressure in his aching cock, he continued to watch her as she bucked and moaned, shivering from the pleasure given by that little silver shaft. He could see clearly as the lips of her pussy opened and closed with each contraction of her orgasm, her back arched, giving him a delicious, teasing glimpses of her luscious ass. Oh god, he was so close to blowing his load just from watching this perfect creature as she pleasured herself. He would just about kill to be in that room right about now.

Could he? Would she welcome him to her bed, appreciate his advances and the option to have a man give her what she so clearly needed right now? Ignoring the niggling voice that told him he did not have the mental facility right now to be making any kind of reasonable decisions, he decided to go into her room and have it out with her right this minute. He had to do something, be it push things to the next level between them—which he knew would be a damning choice, but ignored anyway—or to turn the woman over his knee and teach her the linguistics of reality while under the care of his security in an effort to protect her. Damn it, he had to do something!

With little fear she would see him now, Jason almost ran into the condo. He tossed the sliding door aside, jogged through the living room, and flung open the door to her room. "Kathryn…?"

Looking over in his direction, her eyes still glazed from the nice little orgasm she had just had, the vibrator, still now, in her hand rested on the bed.

"Yes, Jason?" she purred at him.

"I-I heard noises," he stammered his pathetic excuse to enter her room when he knew perfectly well what the noises had been. "Are you okay? Is there something you need?"

"Yes, Jason. I'm all right." Her husky, sated voice alone proved almost enough to bring him to his knees at this point.

"Oh, okay." He stammered as he began to close the door; cursing himself for even thinking his move could get him anywhere with her. After watching her, he was obviously not in his right mind. What in the hell had made him run in there like that? He was obviously delirious, tired, over-worked...whatever. His mind flew over the excuses he could give himself for his unusual behavior, coming up short at every turn.

"Jason, I do actually need something." Her voice stopped him cold. He glanced back across the room at her, seeing her crystal blue eyes, hazed with endorphins, staring directly at him. Her body reclined lazily on the bed, uncovered, glistening with sweat, both from the heat of the night and from her little adventure with herself.

His cock still sat rock solid in his jeans, the top two buttons remained undone. He looked at her, thinking he must be nuts. She was not really asking...he must be imagining it.

As she slipped her pink tongue over her lips, coating them with glistening moisture, she gave him a knowing look. "May I have some water?"

"Yes, ma'am." His heart beating quickly, he wondered if she had seen him at the window, known he'd watched her. He stood there, dumbstruck at her request. Here he was, hard as a rock, ready to do her bidding–anything she asked, especially after her little show–and she wanted water? On her bed, perfectly naked, legs slightly spread providing a tantalizing view of a hint of swollen pink pussy and a portion of her generous round ass, she seriously asked for a drink?

With a little laugh she looked at him, "Jason?"

Jason shook his head, trying desperately to rid himself of the mental images racing through him. She hadn't yet tried in any way to cover herself from his view: her nakedness, the dripping wet sex toy she held. Surely she wanted him to see, to tease him. He couldn't afford to keep thinking this way or it'd be the death of him.

Cursing, he ripped his gaze off her lounging form and pivoted on the thick heel of his boot. Leaving the door open, he walked quickly away. Going to the refrigerator he opened it with such force the door audibly protested before he grabbed a bottle of water. Women! Damn things can get a man in so much trouble! Now he knew he definitely had to leave this job. In fact, I ain't waiting till the morning shift arrives neither! He was angry now, at himself, not her.

As the company's best man, he knew better. She'd proved a very difficult job as his co-workers had warned him, but he had never failed a job. Grabbing his cell phone he punched in his boss's number.

Pete, while also his best friend, was his boss and the owner of the protective services company he worked for. The man was very explicit and stern on the rules he'd created for his protection, for his employees, and the protection of the clients, but most importantly, the protection of the business. Under no circumstances whatsoever were those rules to ever be broken. Jason knew he had really fucked up big time, and for what? A glimpse of the Senator's full-figured, twenty-year-old daughter playing with herself? Simply because she also happened to be the most attractive woman he'd met this side of the border? Besides, her attitude left far too much to be desired, and he was sick of the shopping and the dining out in fancy, high-class restaurants where his jeans and cowboy boots were completely out of place. He was done watching as she slipped the Stewards a Benjamin Franklin when they huffed and puffed over her companion's dinner wear.

He and Pete had just been discussing the possibility of a partnership between the two of them. Shit!

Punching in the number, he thought of Pete's wife and his friend, struggling with the loss of her mother on the very eve of their first child's rough entry into the world. Shit. His hand automatically snapped the lid closed on the phone. Nope, he couldn't do this to Pete. Time to suck it up and stop being such a whiny bitch. He could handle this. He was a professional, damn it! He could do this. With some serious effort, he would tame back the illogical responses this woman seemed to bring out in him, the way being around her screwed with his senses enough to allow him to border on completely insane. To counter the sting, he promised himself some much needed R&R & RW–rest, relaxation, and rigorously working his ass off at the ranch when this job was finished. He firmly decided the temporary loss of his mental capacity was a one-time thing, meant nothing, and tomorrow he'd be back to his old, cold, hard-working self. The pampered life he'd been experiencing while following this filly around town to cater to her indulgences had rubbed off on him. Yup, that was it. Too much of the niceties in life could make any man lose his mind, fast. He'd get over that shit, quick!

Now he only had to convince his body to believe what he had already convinced his mind. No problem there. He was used to being completely in control.

## CHAPTER THREE

Jason had been acting different around her the last few days since he'd walked in on her naked, post masturbation. Stand-offish. Cold. Distant. Uninterested. She clicked off the adjectives in her head. The more he acted like the others before him, like she was a bitch to barely be tolerated, the more she acted like one. Irritated, she thought nothing of taking it out on him. The sting of not being able to even entice a bodyguard she ignored, or paid back by making him take her everywhere that she could dream of to go, gulled at her. She'd bought more the last few days than she had when she'd been with all of her other guards combined. Of course, none of them had led her to erotic daydreams and raging lust to the point of having to pleasure herself, not to mention the desperate display she'd made of herself after. She's tried to call him in like a siren, but he'd done exactly as he should have. He'd kept his distance despite the display she'd made of herself. That cut deep.

Even now, seeing the glazed over look in his eyes as he played with his food after a few hours of waiting for her to get a massage, then her nails done, a full work up at the spa, all she could do was attempt to think of ways to piss him off. He ticked her off, so she paid it forward with robust determination. She'd ordered for them both from the salad of heirloom tomatoes, to the seared tuna, to the crème fraiche he now pushed around. He couldn't have looked more uncomfortable in the dinner jacket she had forced him to wear to adhere to the dress policy of the restaurant.

While she should have been pleased with

herself, should have been thrilled with the way she'd repaid Jason's nonchalant attitude–and bursting with glee at her accomplishment–instead, she felt let down, which only fueled her anger. A weight remained, slowing her heartbeat, rolling like a brick in her stomach. He hadn't even attempted small talk like he had in the past, at least asking her about growing up, school, the last few years since she'd been out. She'd taken his interest, obligation or not, for granted. While there had never been much to truly tell, she'd exercised her mind and made up some good shit each time. Or, so she'd thought. He'd at least seemed amused by her then. Now that he'd seen her naked, he couldn't even look her way despite the fact he obviously couldn't have been less interested in the golden, sugary cream he scooped up only to watch it slide back down off his spoon into the bowl.

"Eat, damn it!" she hissed at him across the table, her tone low but forceful. Her anger laced words normally would have made any man cower. Yet Jason sat looking bored to death and entirely unaffected by her viscous display.

"Look, Kathryn, you can make me stand outside of spa doors all day long while you make yourself relaxed and beautiful. You can force me to wear ridiculous looking, restrictive suits. You can even order my food for me for presentation sake. But, you can not make me put food in my mouth, chew, or swallow. A man has to have some boundaries. Besides, I'm saving my taste buds, and my hunger, for some wings and beer when we get back to the condo."

He'd talked to the dessert rather than her, but she'd received his message loud and clear, though many of the words had been fuzzy, hard to understand, after he'd called her beautiful. Well, technically he'd said 'make herself beautiful', but that meant he thought at some point she could be, right? Maybe. Possibly. It was the first hint she'd gotten from him in days that he thought anything of her at all. Regardless, rather than this fact elating her, raising her mood, it seemed to fuel her bitterness. Something about his comment, an emotion she couldn't identify, made her eyes begin to burn before unexpected tears welled up in the corners. If he'd been paying any attention to her at all, he would have noticed. Thankfully, he'd already returned to ignoring her again.

She tried to pull it together, biting her tongue to avoid lashing out at him. For some reason her cuts, witty comebacks, all remained frozen in her brain, unwilling to show themselves. When an audible groan bordering on a sigh escaped her throat, she grabbed her napkin up off her lap so fast she could feel the rake of her nails, perfectly painted today, across her thigh through her sundress. She carelessly, so unlike her, put the napkin to her eye to dab at the emerging tears that she caught his attention at just the wrong moment. She fumed as he looked at her, mouth hanging open like he'd realized for the first time she was a real girl, with real emotions and all.

This infuriated her. She never let anyone see her innermost thoughts and feelings, not even herself, whoever the hell she was. She knew her role, had learned it at school, and she played it well. So well, in fact, it was who she'd become.

The role she played was all she knew of herself. Tears were never, under any circumstances, allowed.

"Kathryn?" He reached across the table only to hover his calloused hand inches above hers for a moment before he pulled it back.

"Don't act concerned. I have something in my eye. Must have been that stupid lady who did my makeup," she tried to cover.

"What, she got something in both of your eyes over an hour ago that is just now bothering you?"

"A delayed reaction, asshole. Take me home. Or to that hell hole you call a condo so I can wash this shit off my face," she demanded.

When he didn't move, just sat there dumbfounded, she pushed back her chair, purposely making the legs scratch across the floor, hoping she could walk to his side of the table and actually appear threatening. Like she could truly move the mountain of muscle that made up Jason with any physical effort. Her daddy's wallet could, though, and she intended to use that to her advantage. Before she could grab his arm and dig in her fingernails to make him stand, he did so on his own, moving his arm in tight to his body to avoid her touching him at all.

Asshole. The word deafening, even just said internally.

## Chapter Four

Jason had to remind himself about his duty to his friend, Pete, and his job every time this woman made him come close to losing his mind again. She had a knack of getting under his skin whether with her words or her looks. While two completely different types of irritation, he often existed on the edge of his breaking point either way. Between wanting to put her in her place and fuck her, the dominant male in him could only dream of a sexy as hell discipline session. Yet, the internal fight to keep such thoughts far from repeatedly flowing through his head remained alive and well.

When he pulled the car up outside of the place they stayed, she got out immediately, yet again disobeying another simple order to stay in the car until he secured the perimeter and let her out. He took in their surroundings fast, too fast, as he followed her to the door. He had the keys, so even being a few steps behind her, the woman suddenly moving like she ran a sprint, she'd have to stop at the door. Then he could guard her body with his, careful not to get too close. Tedious, but necessary. The whole idea of being so close to her just about undid him, the familiar pulse that turned to an ache in his groin beginning when she slipped through the door.

"Fuck," he yelled, preceded by his screaming out "Kathryn," as his run became a leap through the entranceway.

It had been open, and no one but him and Pete had a key to this place. Pete would never stop by unannounced to a house with an armed guard in it. Jason rapidly scanned the living room as

Kathryn disappeared into her bedroom, slamming the door behind her.

"Damn it, Kathryn," he yelled as he made his way to her door. He didn't bother to knock, his adrenaline fueling him, pushing him instinctively into his training, making him a protector, her bodyguard first and foremost.

He entered the room accompanied by the soundtrack of her scream. His entrance precipitated a brief struggle between her and her attacker she easily lost. With his gun raised, aimed, finger poised over the trigger, he couldn't get a clean shot as the man used Kathryn like a shield. While the intruder struggled to move them both toward the already open window, which seemed odd given someone had broken in through the front door, Jason used the mirror to form a plan of attack to take the man down without harming his charge. Then he saw the message taped to the mirror, a threat that her attacker would soon take her.

This was all a game to this man. He obviously didn't want to harm Kathryn, just scare her and her father. He was smart. Had made his way past the secured front door. He'd taken too stereotypical of a way of leaving a threat on the mirror, all in large cutout letters from various sources, and had probably been about to leave through the window he'd opened when Kathryn had stupidly stormed in on him. He'd clearly only tried to make a point that if he wanted to, he could do something. What he really wanted, his demands, would come next. All the man probably sought now was a clean exit. Devoid of a clear shot without endangering Kathryn, Jason hoped his theory was correct.

He remained poised, gun aimed if he got a chance at a shot, as the man shuffled them to the window, his arm tight about Kathryn's throat. Moving cautiously, Jason remained only a few inches away from them, ready to take a bullet for her if this creep drew a gun. He only cared that he could grab her once the man tried to exit out the window. Under no circumstances would this man take her from him, even if he had to die to pull it off. Ready as the stalker moved to step out the window, he found himself catching Kathryn as the stalker thrust her at him. The man's violent push sent her slamming into him so fast he had to stiffen his hand, take the impact of her body against his fingers on his gun without firing the weapon he'd been poised to shoot. A damn difficult maneuver, even for him.

Without conscious thought, acting on pure instinct alone, he wrapped his free arm around her to secure her to him as he turned them both, putting his body not only between her and the stalker in case he decided to take a shot, but also between her and the ground they were soon to hit. And, hit they did, with a heavy thud. His ass hit the ground, his back the windowsill, and her body crushed his against both surfaces. He reached through the pain to pull down the window with an aching hand, still miraculously holding his gun, but he couldn't reach. He rolled to the side, pushed her to the ground, covered her with his body, and cautiously peered out the window.

In the dark night, even with the streetlights, Jason watched the assailant get into a nondescript, dark colored car across the street. Slamming the window shut so hard Kathryn screamed again, he locked it back up. Of course, while they had special locks, the glass reinforced so it couldn't be broken, this guy had entered through the front door, so opening the window had been nothing from the inside. He would have to inspect the front door to ascertain the skills this guy retained that he had so easily gotten inside the specialty locks. The man was a pro with a point to make. The message given tonight, Jason had received loud and clear. The stalker hadn't wanted to hurt her this time or he would have, but there was no telling what he would do the next. Plus, he kept getting to them. He had proof now, he believed, that an internal leak had led this guy to them once again. He needed to take her, get her out of here now.

The thought had barely entered his brain when a plan started to form. Screw policy. He'd keep her safe. He'd take her with him to his ranch. He'd tell no one where they'd gone, only tell Pete she would remain safe in an undisclosed location.

They could fire him after the stalker had been caught. He'd gladly give up the job. He could check in from time to time on burner phones until they managed to catch the man, but until then they would both disappear. That is all he would tell Pete, his plan.

But first, he had to comfort the sobbing woman trembling in his arms, snuggled into his body.

"It's over, Kathryn. You are okay. But, you broke the rules running from the car without me and paid a horrible price. I'm taking you away from here, somewhere where I know I can keep you safe until they catch this guy. You need to grab your stuff so we can leave now. We are open targets with the front door compromised, probably unable to be locked again. I will stand here, make a phone call while you grab your stuff as fast as you can."

He tried to stand, but she only shook her head as she continued to vibrate in his arms. She had a death grip on his sides, getting clothing and flesh, her thick, manicured nails leaving crescent shaped indentations just below his ribs.

"Kathryn. Please. I have you. You are safe. But, sweetheart, we have to move fast before the guy comes back." Even though he didn't believe the man would dare at this point, Jason needed to scare her into understanding as he pushed her away from him, easily overpowering her death-like grip on him so he could look her in the eyes. "Can you do that for me? Can you grab just what you need?"

She nodded, her red-rimmed eyes wide with fear.

"Good. Do so while I make a call to my boss, tell him a brief description of my plan."

He figured he could leave his phone here after the call. They would be completely out of touch until after he had secured them at the ranch and gone out to buy a burner and check in again. He only told Pete they were going to disappear before hanging up on the man. Next he called the head of staff at the ranch, instructing them that while he was coming there, if anyone called they were to say they had not heard from him. Then he wiped the calls from the log, did a fast factory reset, and turned off the phone purposefully tossing it on her bed. With bag in her hand, he pulled her to him again. Tucked under his side for her protection, they moved cautiously into every room, his gun aimed, held steady despite a painfully bruised hand.

As he pulled away from the curb, her with her head down below the dashboard, he wished he could focus on the fact that somewhere Pete was cursing him up and down right now. He'd left his friend with the message to catch this bastard stalker and then he would return her home. Pete knew about the ranch, but his employees would make sure no one knew he was actually there. Kathryn and he would literally go off grid, hiding in the most obvious place due to the help of a loyal staff who had already been carefully instructed for years lest he ever need such a backup plan to disappear. They had protocol even if someone showed up in person to the ranch. When the order was given, they knew their first and most important responsibility was to keep him hidden there.

He wished he could be concerned with Pete's anger. Instead, as he drove through the night, rushing Kathryn to safety, all he could think about were the nerve endings still awake and tingling all over him from where her body had pressed against his.

CHAPTER FIVE

It had been dark when they arrived at Jason's ranch yesterday, and Kathryn had been unable to get a clear vision of her surroundings, this dream home and ranch Jason had told her about on the way here. Basically, the guy had talked a mile a minute. She figured it had been his attempt to get her mind off what had just happened to her. All she really got from what he said, though, her brain still having trouble with the whole concentration thing, was the fact they were driving a few hours north of Sacramento to a horse ranch he owned. He loved the place. That came out loud and clear. He trusted his staff to hide them in such an obvious location. She understood that, too. She had to trust him.

She appreciated his efforts to distract her, but the 'what ifs' of the whole situation kept pinging around in her brain, causing the dull ache there to grow into an actual throbbing headache. She'd been whisked through the darkness into a spare bedroom and told to sleep. While she convinced herself she never would again, her body had other ideas and she'd promptly acquiesced to a dreamless sleep after the harrowing attack at the condo. She had been beyond exhausted, and thankfully, practically asleep before her head hit the pillow and any other violent images of her wild imagination formed.

Walking out into the bright morning sun now, though, she could see the wood and stone structures that seemed to spring from the surrounding woodland as if organic, made from them and complementing the landscapes if they'd sprung up naturally like a tree or plant. Jason had built this dream home of his on such gorgeous property. The view, unlike any she'd ever experienced before, took her breath away. The rugged landscape, the rustic buildings, it looked like the Wild West in California. It wasn't something she'd ever dreamed of seeing, a horse ranch, but standing here she realized how her pre-judgments of ranch life had led her to really miss out. She felt right at home, oddly, and she'd truly never felt that before; not in her father's huge, exquisitely decorated house, or at the stuffy and regimented boarding school.

The canopy of trees and growth of wildflowers, barely blooming anymore at beginning of summer, along the well-worn path to the stables had kept her from seeing any of the creatures she could hear moving around her. She was extremely grateful for the dense foliage as her mind conjured up horrific critters, more like mutant animals, out to make her part of their early morning meal. Of course, not seeing them, not knowing if they were perhaps only an adorable squirrel rustling for nuts, or a colorful bird disturbing the leaves as it hopped from branch to branch in search of food for her young, may have made it worse. She had no real idea what could be out here. Wolf? Bear? What animals did live out here? The thoughts made her quicken her pace, and a flush of relief swept through her as the stables came into view. She had pictured a small building with a few horses, but instead a high-end facility teaming with activity loomed before her.

Avoiding a few curious glances her way from other ranch hands, she covered her mouth to suffuse the smell of manure as she made her way into the barn in search of Jason. He'd left her a note saying where he was, but he'd be back to check on her before breakfast. She probably should have stayed put, waited from him in the cozy house, but curiosity had overwhelmed logic. Walking around the house, she'd decided apparently the guy did have taste after all, in spades. Even though the huge and spacious house was done in warm woods with the contrast of clean, crisp whites, things like strategically placed art and a bright red western throw brought it all together, made the place feel classy and homey at the same time. From the huge kitchen, equipped to cook for a restaurant full of people, to the library with floor to ceiling bookshelves, and the massive, fully decked out game room, the house had so much to offer. She felt like she may never want to leave before the reality of that thought struck her and she shook her head at her absurd notions, following her mounting curiosity outdoors.

With what she'd seen so far, she was glad she had. She just couldn't get over how comfortable she felt in a place that couldn't be more foreign to her had she travel far overseas, though she had only been driven a few hours out of the city. The stables were something. She stood on a red brick floor looking down a corridor of stalls with doors made of warm colored wood that matched the house, with black iron bars you could see the horses through. The walls and ceiling were made up of the same wood. Even the freaking stables were immaculately decorated with what appeared to be antique equipment hanging from the walls.

Walking a few feet into the stable, despite the brief stares of stable hands, she found Jason brushing down a heavily pregnant, great black mare in one of the stalls. She stood for a moment in awe of his obviously practiced care of the animal. He stroked her flank firmly, all the while murmuring soothing sounds that seemed to be more random noises than words.

"Hey," she spoke softly, not wanting to spook either horse or master.

Jason visibly tensed as her voice met his ears, and he responded with a curt, "Hi. You should have stayed in the house. Jeanette was instructed to provide you anything you needed. Is there something you need even she couldn't grant?"

Embarrassment, hot and heavy, rushed through her, a flush creeping up her face despite her, but she sighed. "No. I don't need anything, Jason. Never mind. Thank you."

She pivoted on her boot heel and took a step back in the direction she'd come, then pulled up short when Jason's firm, calloused hand closed over her arm, spinning her back around to face him.

"I'm sorry. I didn't mean for that to come out so abrupt. Last night left me a bit out of it. Tired. Rest assured, though, I met with my staff once we arrived, and we went through the whole plan for them to hide us here. No one who calls or even shows up will be allowed to know we are actually here. Besides, Pete would assume this was the last place I would bring you. I trust my staff completely, so I hope you will too." He ran a hand through his dark hair, slicking it back with the sweat already beaded on his forehead. "You ride, or are those just for show?" He gestured to her calf-length leather boots with a half-smile softening his features.

Kathryn's heart leapt at the sight of the smile and she grinned, "Yes, Jason, as amazing as it may seem, I actually can ride a horse," she responded flippantly. "In fact, it's one of the things I enjoyed most in my off time at school, and I've become pretty good at it. I ride English, not western, and have been trained a bit for competitive riding. But, how different could it all be, right?"

"Then we will ride. I'll be right back." He flashed her a quick glance of his white, even teeth before he strode into the barn leading the mare.

Watching his retreating back, his ass encased in dark jeans stretched across wide hips, she wondered if there were any angle she didn't find him drool-worthy. As he returned leading two smaller horses, one a beautiful mahogany, the other a pale white, she answered her own question. No.

CHAPTER SIX

Before they set out across the acres of lush, green fields, he gave her a brief lesson in the round pen in the transition from English to Western riding. While mainly a difference in the contact of the rider and horse, she seemed willing to learn and picked it up easily. The appearance of her genuine interest intrigued him. He'd never seen her actually excited about doing anything, unless it was to shop, spa, and dine; all in places that may as well have been foreign lands speaking foreign languages to him. The way she seemed to cling to every word he said with her undivided attention did something to him, let him see a different side of her he didn't even realize existed. Maybe another side did exist within this woman other than the one her life had created. Maybe she didn't even realize it existed within her. He didn't know if he would be happy or scared to find she actually had a depth of character hidden somewhere deep within, given the physical attraction he already had for her. If she became nice, easy-going, and interested in the same things, he might just be a goner, losing any self-control her former attitude had helped him hang on to, even if only just by a thread.

After the hasty lesson, they rode easily through trails formed only by use: the hooves of the horses, and the boots of man this far out onto his eighteen hundred acre ranch. They didn't really talk, as he more enjoyed watching her take pleasure in the ride, having an excuse to keep looking at her under the guise of making sure she was doing okay. She sat a beautiful picture on the gorgeous animal beneath her. With the backdrop of the trees, the mountains in front of them, he found it all quite breathtaking, but nothing seemed to get under his skin, pleasure his senses more than her. He was so in trouble. Maybe bringing her out here to a place where no one knew where they were wasn't the greatest idea, especially considering his urges where she was concerned, but what choice did he have? If anyone actually did call looking for him, he'd at least have time to make them disappear on the property if need be.

He felt safe here. No one who worked for Pete knew he had this place, so no one would be able to guess where he'd taken her without doing some serious digging.

Side by side they followed a winding creek just below the gentle rise of the land. It had been this small trickle of water that had sold him on the place, thus inspiring him to name the ranch, Major's Creek. They rode along the bubbling brook for some time before he suggested it was time they make their way back. Back through the tall, green prairie grasses, fields that only a month ago were an unending blanket of bluebonnets around the limestone outcroppings. Her smile seemed to grow larger, a glow traveling through her face until the happiness shone in her eyes as she took in the scenery. She even asked him questions about the ranch, what he did here, her true interest in his home shooting an arrow right to his heart that got that whole groin area all worked up again, too.

They were close to the stables again, outside the covered arena, when he spotted a partially downed fence. Old, the whole thing needing replacing in this section. While the ranch hands would fix it before working out any of the horses in the space, he had an urge to handle it himself. He'd been away from the ranch too long, and with all of the lust coursing through him lately, he needed to work with his hands a bit. Pounding a nail with a hammer just sounded good. It seemed like a logical solution to the energy brimming inside him.

"Listen, I need to get this fence fixed, so I'll take you back. One of the hands will care for the horse, and I will see you later at the house. I had someone run this morning and get us a couple of burner phones so you can get ahold of me anytime you need to. They are at the stables, set up with each other's numbers on emergency dial, so I'll make sure you get one before you go back to the house."

"Do you mind if I just stay with you?" she asked him, shocking him with the softness of her voice. She actually asked him a question, sought his permission, rather than simply demanding him to do something or outright refusing to do what he'd asked.

"Listen, Kathryn, I know yesterday was scary but you are safe here. No one knows where we are, not even my boss. I ditched my phone, so no one tracked us here. And my staff, whom I trust implicitly, all know as much as they need to, enough to know they need to keep their eyes peeled."

"It's not that. I mean, yes, yesterday was terrifying, and I appreciate all you did, and all you are doing for me. It's just...I would rather stay outdoors...with you. I don't really want to sit inside the house bored to tears. I just can't get over how beautiful this land is. I would rather stay here and stare at the landscape while you fix the fence than anything I could do in the house. Besides, surely I'll have plenty of time at night to explore the library and play in the game room."

He stood there a minute, dumbfounded, looking into her face, trying to reconcile her expression with the words that had come out of her mouth. Not whiny, not demanding, just normal, soft with a touch of husky woman tone. This whole persona switch was throwing him for a loop and he was still unsure how to handle it.

"Uh, well, I didn't take you for the outdoorsy type."

"Who knew," she mused with a giggle, the sound of it vibrating through him, sending another spark of longing below his belt.

"If you're sure you won't be bored, then sure, you can stay. Wait here a minute for me to go grab what I need. I'll be right back," he ordered as he noticed one of his ranch hands moving toward them, out inspecting the fence.

He clicked his tongue and with a slight pull on the reins, he encouraged his mount to turn and shift into a fast trot, intent on stopping the guy from getting too close to Kathryn, lest she overhear he didn't actually need to fix the fence himself. His staff all listened well, and they were used to him pitching in, so he received little argument from the young hand about wanting to do the work on the fence.

Once inside the tool and tack barn, he made short work of grabbing the gear he needed, and then found himself rushing back to be with her. He wanted to experience more of this new version of Kathryn, lest she vanish as quickly as she appeared. The ranch was a magical place. It had certainly transformed his life, so maybe it would have a positive impact on this spoiled little rich girl, too. It would make his job easier in a way, but could make keeping his distance more difficult.

He granted her a brief smile upon his return, finding her standing beside her horse, holding the reins with one hand, absently petting the stallion with her other as she stared off in a sleepy-looking daze around her. A smile, not big, but genuine, soft and beautiful graced her features and lit up her eyes. He found he couldn't look away.

He stopped on his horse right beside her, catching her attention again.

"This place is amazing. You are lucky to have it," she gushed.

"Thank you," he mumbled as he dismounted, still getting used to this new adaptation of the previously annoying woman he'd spent his last few weeks with.

"Don't act so surprised," she huffed, although there was more teasing than an edge to her voice.

"Sorry. I just figured you to be the type to be more impressed by a mansion with a giant pool than a ranch house with a small lake."

"I would have thought so, too. The places I rode were always so manicured: covered arenas, a few well cared for trails that more resembled a golf course setting. It wasn't really like being outdoors. Not like this anyway. I've never experienced such a majestic scene as this," she said as she gestured out over the land.

"Well, I'm glad you like it because there are no malls nearby, unless you count a strip mall of sorts around the farmers market. Along with that, the only places to eat are mom and pop owned, homegrown cooking, and there is no telling how long you are going to be stuck here," he said, getting out his tools and getting to work. "Jeanette is an amazing cook, though she tends to be more steak and apple pie than whatever the hell you ordered us at that last restaurant."

"I don't mind. Honestly. I want to experience everything here, find out what it's like to really live in a place like this. Feel like I should apologize—"

"No need," he said, cutting her off. "There is no need at all. I think I get it."

"I don't know what you get, but you are the first bodyguard who didn't look to ditch me, gratefully ditch me, as soon as the stalker showed up again. Anyway," she said with a noticeable shudder passing through her shoulders. Her brows furrowed, she nodded to the fence. "Think I could help?"

"With what?" he said, following her nod with a raised eyebrow. "You don't seriously mean with mending the fence?"

"Yes, I do indeed mean the fence. Why not? I'm sure I could learn to use that stuff you brought." Her indignant attitude showed through briefly at his doubt, but disappeared just as quickly.

"Stuff as in tools? A hammer and nails? Well, I'm sure you could do anything you set your stubborn mind to, but if you mess up that new manicure of yours there is nowhere to get a new one out here."

"I'll live. I think," she said, and followed with a giggle.

He couldn't read her right now. She appeared to be engaged in some internal struggle to prove herself capable of anything she set her mind to. Enjoying the moment, and her clear attempt at wanting to at least try, he agreed to let her help.

First he gave her a lesson on a nail and a hammer. He was old school in caring for the place because he loved it that way. He stood behind her and wrapped his hands around her waist, showing her how to best position her feet so she didn't topple off balance on the first try. Leaning in he tucked himself against her back, burying his nose in her hair for a moment before giving himself a mental shake.

Grasping her right hand in his, he slid her fist down the smooth shaft of the hammer, "No, grab it here, firmly, or you'll get no drive behind it and end up hurting your wrist in the process. You have to be careful at first, just tap the nail enough to initially push it into the wood. Do it gently while you are holding it, in case you miss and hit your thumb. Still going to hurt, though, I warn you, so go slow and careful. After it's in enough to be stable, you can move your fingers and really pound away at the thing," he said, chuckling at the sexual analogy that snuck into his head with those words.

Her heat combined with the scent of cinnamon

and vanilla wafting to his nostrils made his cock thicken behind his zipper. He took a quick step back before he embarrassed himself. "Here, watch me a moment."

She attentively watched him work on the first nail, and then gave it an earnest try herself. They laughed at her repeated mistakes, tears springing to her eyes the one time she did end up smashing her thumb instead of the nail. She'd powered through it though, to his amazement, and then chatted about the different tools, their uses, types of wood used in the fence and found surrounding the ranch, until they managed to finally repair the enclosure together. The mending took longer than it would have had he done it alone. Yet somehow teaching her these menial tasks, knowing she was literally hanging on his every word and truly learning what he was showing her, well, the feeling of a job well done bloomed throughout him. He felt quite good about it.

Her excitement was contagious, as if the same feeling of accomplishment written across her face increased his. She was so proud of herself and it showed. He wondered briefly if anyone had ever taken the time to be with her like this, hands on, really teach her to do something other than just dictating what she should learn from across the room. His full attention quickly transferred from the internal monologue back to her, captured by her full breasts swaying as she bounced a little. She radiated inner pleasure with herself at this very moment, a true satisfaction with her own ability to do such a simple task. The look on her face broadcast something he'd never seen from her before. A small bit of confidence. Minor, no doubt, as she'd spent most of her life obviously bereft of such a feeling, but there nonetheless.

He had the urge to celebrate her new found happiness by pulling her to him in a hug that would squish those generous globes against his firm chest and allow him to breathe in more of her delicious fragrance. A sharp, hot rush shot through his belly to his groin, making him grow hard just at the thought. Instead, he shook his head, pushing the idea of such an intimate gesture away fast, and flashed a smile at her.

"Who are you? And, what have you done with Kathryn?" he teased, or at least he attempted to make it sound that way.

"Would you rather I demanded you find the nearest mall, however far away, and take me shopping?" she quipped in return.

"No. No. Not at all. You've just changed so much. Overnight. I recognize the face, the body..." I definitely recognize the luscious body. "But, the voice, the words, they're just throwing me a bit off my game. I no longer want to throw you over my knee and beat your bratty ass. Well I do, but not the same way I did before." He stumbled, realizing the words that had just escaped his mouth. "Shit, did I just say that out loud? It's just a figure of speech. I don't want to make you uncomfortable. I..."

He lost his ability to think as images of his handprint plastered in red across her ass filled his mind. Even with the change, he still wanted to discipline this woman, maybe for all she put him through before, maybe...just because.

"Stop. It's fine. I deserve that. Might not mind

it at all," she said boldly, giving him a wink, though a crimson blush rushed from her neck to her cheeks.

"All right, let's get back." He needed to break this moment, now, before his mind decided to take her as seriously as his dick just had.

He moved to get back on his horse lest she see the aftermath of her flippant comment. He convinced himself she only attempted to tease him back, trying make him feel comfortable, or at least letting him off the hook, whatever her intention. Now, if only the throbbing ache inside his jeans would listen to reason.

## CHAPTER SEVEN

Jeanette had already been cooking a meal by the time they returned to the ranch house, but giving Kathryn a wink, she assured Jason the stew wouldn't be ready until dinner if they needed to go out for a few things, given the hasty pack job Kathryn had been forced to do when they left the condo. The older woman suggested, a sly grin crossing her features, that while they were there they may as well 'sit a bit and have some lunch out.'

Kathryn didn't think she had ever actually

encountered such a genuine kindness by an employee. She didn't appear to want to serve Kathryn, but rather to be actually concerned with her needs. She couldn't explain exactly how she got that impression, but since she had met Jeanette, the woman acted more like she was a best friend trying to essentially, selflessly help. Kathryn assumed this to be the case, anyway, as she had no other experience to explain the anomalies of the way the woman acted. It certainly wasn't something she was used to in her world. She kind of enjoyed the difference, if she were honest.

"I could use a few things," Kathryn said hesitantly, glancing toward Jason, "and I am willing to try some of the local cuisine, though I can't wait to try that stew, too. It smells wonderful, Jeanette."

Jason shot Kathryn an amused, shocked look; again like she was an alien from another planet, or maybe one had taken over her body.

It felt like the right explanation to her. She didn't feel herself at all lately, and really, the changes she felt blossoming inside her appealed to her. She had to admit to being just as shocked as Jason.

"It's settled then. I wouldn't dream of trying to argue with two beautiful, stubborn women. Let me get changed, and we will leave. We can go out the back roads and circle around to avoid any locals seeing me here, though it isn't like Pete is going to ask around town for me once you tell him I'm not here. Actually, we'll go one town over, if you don't mind the drive, where no one knows me by sight, just to play it extra safe."

"Pete's already called," Jeanette said before Kathryn could object with a retort to Jason calling her stubborn. "Said he knew it was a shot in the dark, you were smarter than that, but he was desperate to find you. He said on the off chance I did talk to you, if you called to check in on the ranch, to let you know how pissed Senator Caruthers was to not be privy to where his daughter was. Guess he made all sorts of threats to Pete, demanding he tell him information Pete honestly didn't know. He had to tell him you had gone rogue in the best interests of his daughter and so forth. Man isn't happy."

"Figured as much, but I can't worry about that now. My goal is to keep Kathryn safe. If that means losing the job to do so, or upsetting her father, so be it. Hate to put Pete under so much heat, but he knows me. He will eventually, hopefully, understand why."

"Why would you do that for me?" Kathryn asked, tears filling her eyes despite her best efforts to not let them, to stifle all of these new emotions hitting her all at once since she'd come here.

"I'm committed to the job first. Your safety above all else. I'd been toying with leaving the security detail and doing the ranch full time again anyway. I just hadn't found a way to tell Pete yet. Please don't worry. In the end, once your stalker is caught, and you're safe, I'm sure Pete, and hopefully even your father will be grateful for what I've done. Now, I'm going to get changed. You meet me outside at the truck in a few minutes," he said, turning on his heel to make a hasty exit, leaving both Kathryn and Jeanette standing there, jaws slack with shock at his announcement.

***

By the time Jason met Kathryn at his truck, he could only hope he had talked himself into a safe state to spend more time alone with her. At least out in public he couldn't jump this new edition of Kathryn. Her sudden personality change was taking away his every argument to keep his distance.

She'd changed into an alluring white blouse, overlaid with a light layer of fragile white lace, and a pair of perfectly pressed, designer jeans. She looked angelic as she gracefully climbed into his old truck. He drove the battered beast because he liked it. It suited him. But now, today, it also helped to blend in with the town folk. They could draw no attention to themselves if he wanted to keep her safe, which would be hard enough with the beauty sitting by his side.

"You are staring," she said, drawing him out

of his thoughts.

"Oh, yeah, it's just...well, you look beautiful, and we don't want to draw any attention to ourselves."

"You think I look beautiful," she asked back, her voice catching a little.

"Of course. You always do, and now, here, it is a problem." Especially for me. "Will you protest too loudly if I make you wear one of my cowboy hats? I mean, in an effort not to draw attention to yourself as an outsider, of course. You may not turn as many heads if you wore a cowboy hat and boots, but I don't have boots in your size."

"Well, we can make boots our first stop, then, and I will happily wear your hat now that you have given me such a compliment, even if it was hidden behind a valid reason."

He snapped his gaze back to the road, forcing himself to focus on the dusty gravel as he started the truck. He needed to keep his mind on driving and off thoughts of the way she looked with his hat pressed down over those curly, chestnut locks, or he'd be distracted by the very real fact his jeans would soon not fit over his dick.

Jason drove a little too fast, he knew, and he had to slam on the brakes when they came skidding around a turn to find a truck stopped on a back road in the middle of nowhere. A large, balding, cheesy tattoo-covered man dropped a bulging, black bag just off the side of the road. He'd made fast for his truck, climbing in and peeling away with a shower of gravel and dust in his wake.

Jason suppressed his desire to give chase just as he heard Kathryn shriek and the protesting squeal of her door as it opened fast on rusty hinges. He turned his head to see her jumping out of the truck.

"Have you learned nothing?" he yelled. He slammed the truck gear into park and, with his thoughts flashing back to the condo last night, stumbled hastily out of his side of the vehicle swatting at the choking dust billowing into his face.

He'd just rounded the front of the truck,

coming out of the thick brown-tinged cloud to hear her scream again as she reached forward before losing her footing and falling into a mud puddle. While they hadn't gotten any rain for days, some low lying areas retained their puddles for weeks after a heavy storm. And, of course, in her white, dressy shirt, Kathryn had managed to find one.

As she screamed and screeched, a group of furry, dark colored and very much moving puppies he could now see stopped dead in their tracks. He crouched and gave a short whistle as he accessed the scene before him. Three puppies clumsily made their way up the short embankment to him, probably looking for protection against the crazy lady flapping around in the mud like a drowning woman. A maybe a two inch deep, yet maybe a foot wide all around puddle, and she sounded as if she thought she were dying in a lake. He couldn't help but chuckle at her current predicament. Served her right for defying him and getting out of the truck in the first place.

He was trying to pet the three muddy little heads climbing over one another, vying for his attention, as she finally got to standing. With a few splashes of mud on her face, the most damage had been to the frilly blouse she wore, having landed squarely on her generous chest in the mud.

Seeing her red-faced expression, looking like she was about ready to explode into her usual tirade of nastiness, he suppressed a wide grin as stood and turned to the truck to get a few old rags and a horse blanket he had in the back.

With the puppies in tow, tangling themselves at his feet, he grabbed the items and cautiously approached her.

"I'm so sorry," he said, biting his bottom lip hard, trying to keep the creeping humor from his voice.

"I'm fine," she snipped.

"I'm sure." He offered her a rag. "To at least get some mud off of yourself.

"Traitors," she said to the puppies around him, one still looking around, two sitting quietly at his feet and staring up at her. "How come they came right to you but made me chase them?"

"Exactly, you chased after them, came at them at a run. I was crouching down, not scary at all, when they came to me. Never had a dog, have you?"

"No, I haven't. Not sure I want one now. I was trying to save you, you little monsters, and you lead me into a lake of mud." She thrust out her bottom lip in a pout.

"Well, more like a foot square puddle, but given it is probably your first encounter with one of those, too, I will allow you the over-exaggeration."

"Thank you so much," she hissed as she furiously wiped at her shirt, now a hideous brown shade of streaked white.

"Here, wrap this blanket around you now that you have the majority of the mud off so you don't get my truck a mess."

"You are too kind, sir."

He nodded, not helping her out of fear of proximity, and moved toward the driver's side of the truck

"Wait. Aren't you going to help them?" she demanded.

"They are following me," he snipped back. "So, you want to save this litter of cow dogs?"

"Of course. Why do you think I got out of the truck in the first place? Though I don't really know what possessed me. Look where it got me."

"Well, I'll be damned, Kathryn Caruthers, you do have a heart after all," he said, knowing his own heart was now a goner. "We'll have to take them back to the barn, though, and postpone our outing."

CHAPTER EIGHT

"Oh my God! They are so adorable!" Kathryn squealed and squatted, reaching for the bitch lying in the hay nursing her pups.

"Kathryn, no!" Jason grabbed her elbow and yanked her backward just as the protective mother growled and nipped out in warning. "You never, never go near a momma and her babies that way, and certainly not when she's feeding or as fast as you did. Animals are protective of their young, and any sudden move in their direction is perceived as an immediate threat. Great way to get your hand bitten, woman!"

She leaned back into Jason as he held her tight to his chest with a protective arm wrapped around her middle. She could feel the heat emanating off his skin and a strong throbbing in his chest pressing repeatedly against the cool, dampness of the blouse covering her back. She'd actually scared him enough to make his heart pound? The knowledge melted a part of her she didn't even know she had inside. Emotions slammed into her, hard, knocking her mentally off balance and sending her thoughts racing through her mind. He cared. Jason really and truly cared about her well being, and in the face of even the smallest danger he reacted to protect her. This wasn't just about the job. Her Daddy's money wasn't the driving force behind his actions anymore. The idea that someone actually cared about her sent a shock through her body that traveled its way to her core in a rush of heat.

"I've had it!" Jason was still clearly very angry as he grabbed her hand and dragged her out of the stall. "You need a lesson you won't soon forget, young lady. Every time I am stupid enough to step a foot from you for more than a single damn second you put yourself in harm's way. Enough is enough!"

She cringed at the tone in his voice. Jason actually yelling at her, anyone yelling at her for that matter, was more than unexpected, it was literally unheard of.

"Now listen here, Jason. No one, and I mean no one raises—" Her words were sharply cut off as he sat on a hay bale and dragged her facedown over his lap.

"No, you listen, missy. This is the very last time you will disobey my orders and go running off willy nilly into a dangerous situation, do you hear me," he roared at her.

Struggling to push herself upright, she whined back at him, "Jason, let me go."

"Nope, sorry, not this time, pretty lady." He hooked his leg over her jean-clad knees, effectively trapping her over his lap. No matter how much she struggled, Kathryn couldn't get free.

"I've had more than I can take from you, and it's high time you learned what happens to those who misbehave."

Shock registered as his large, firm hand came down hard on her backside. "Jason! What the hell do you—" Another slap rang out in the otherwise quiet barn and she could hear Jason's breathing getting heavy, faster as he panted out obscenities. Each word was enforced by another crack to her now warming ass.

"You. Will. Not. Put. Yourself. In. Danger."

Kathryn felt a blush of heat infuse her face, trailing down her neck to her chest, just as the high temperature spread out over her bruising bottom and down her thighs, sending a rush of moisture to her core. She felt mortified to be in this position. How dare he treat me like a child! Sputtering and attempting her best to wiggle away from his forceful punishment, Kathryn wasn't sure if she were more disgusted by the fact she was being spanked, or her response to his manhandling and objectification.

Jason raged on, "You. Will. Take. Better.

Care. Of. Yourself. Young. Lady."

It was clear to her she'd crossed some line, though she truly didn't understand what, and he didn't seem to be slowing any as her buttocks now began a throbbing, searing burn. Tears sprung to her eyes against her will, and for the first time in forever Kathryn couldn't contain them and had no choice but to let them fall.

She stilled her movements, became docile and prone over his legs, no longer fighting the spanking as tears tracked down her face and dropped into the hay on the floor of the barn. The contrast of emotions running through her at this moment sucked away her very breath. Here she was, lying over the lap of her protector like an errant child, getting her ass tanned six ways from Sunday–honestly the first time she had ever been spanked in her life–and yet she was reacting to it as if he'd stroked her intimately.

"I'm...sorry, Jason," Kathryn sobbed out. "I will behave, I swear.

The words seemed to take the wind out of his sails as Jason suddenly stopped, rubbing her bottom gently with the palm of his hand, trailing his fingers between the waistband of her jeans and her ruined shirt.

"Shhhh, it's okay. I know, baby," he cooed at her. "I lost my temper there for a bit, not something that happens often, let me tell you, and I think maybe now you just may not be so quick to put yourself in the line of fire so often. You know, for a spoiled brat you sure don't think of yourself much when it comes to real danger. You're great at pampering and fine dining, but you haven't a clue how to stay the hell away from situations that could cause you real harm. I guess it finally got to me, and this is the only way I could think of to get it into that lovely brain of yours." Jason slid his leg off her knees and helped her to a sitting position beside him on the bale.

Sniffling, Kathryn winced at the tenderness of her butt cheeks as she placed her substantial weight on them. "I don't know why you even care, Jason. Other than Daddy's money and the hefty amount you're sure to receive as long as you return me in one piece, what's the big deal?"

Jason stood and walked to the door of the stall where the new mother had welcomed the three abandoned pups as if they were her own. His back was rigid, his form completely unyielding as he let lose with a long, drawn out groan. "Kathryn, it's complicated. I apologize for the way I handled your discipline, but you seriously had it coming and I couldn't help myself any longer. I've watched you endanger yourself time and time again these last few weeks, and one can only imagine how you've made it this far in life without serious injury or worse. You needed a reality check, simple, and that's all it was. You got it, now maybe, just maybe you will think twice before getting yourself into anymore trouble."

Kathryn wiped the remaining tears and snot from her face with the muddied sleeve of her shirt, noticing she now had a slash in the fabric to go along with the smelly smears, and hoped she didn't look quite as horrible as she currently felt.

Feeling bold at his words, knowing this man actually cared for her as more than just a charge to be protected, gave her a confidence she'd never felt before. She decided it was now or never, she had to take the chance or she may end up walking out of here regretting it forever when all this stalker business was over with. Besides, this throbbing between her legs was killing her and there was something she could choose to do about it. Please. Let this work. Don't let me get shot down or I swear I will never, ever approach a man again. Time to take matters into my own hands, or in this case, hopefully Jason's hands, and for once in my life really take what I want, what I need.

Kathryn sighed loudly, and then straightening her spine, pushing her shoulders back in determination, she nodded even though she knew he wouldn't see. She pushed herself up off the hay bale and took two cautious steps in his direction, gathering her courage even more. "You're right, Jason. I promise to take better care of myself from now on. To be more aware of what is going on around me. I intend to live life like I've never lived it before," she resolved.

"Starting right now."

***

He felt Kathryn slip her cool palms up his firm back, tracing the tight muscles that ran beneath his shoulder blades. He sucked in his breath as her full breasts pressed into his back and she slid her hands around his sides, down over his firm stomach, then down to his jeans and his cock, only slightly hard now.

Her breath in his hair at the back of his neck sent shivers down his spine and made his cock thicken so quickly it actually hurt him.

"I'm hungry, Jason," she said against his neck, leaving no doubt about the nature of her hunger.

"I'm trying to control myself, Kathryn, but…" He pressed his lips together as her teeth scraped across his neck. "A man has limits."

"I don't want you to control yourself, Jason." She dug her long, polished fingernails through his shirt to press roughly into his hips.

He hissed and spun around, grabbing her wrists in his large hand and holding them firm.

"Kathryn," He warned, the threat obvious in his gruff tone.

She gave him such a longing, innocent look he almost melted there and then.

Holding her wrists tightly, he started to push her away from him.

She twisted suddenly and her ass was then at a level with his groin, her arms now wrapped around herself with his hugging her. She rubbed her full ass up and down over his hips, moving in such a way the friction of his jeans against his hard, throbbing cock sent little electric shocks through him, making him almost lose his mind with the pleasure.

He leaned forward, inhaling the scent of her clean-smelling, mahogany hair mixed with the musty smell of mud and grass. "You need to get out of these wet clothes, take a shower. Your Daddy will have my head on a platter if any harm comes to you out here."

"Please, Jason. Stop pushing me away. I know what I want, what I need." She leaned back into his chest, her heat all but scorching even through the wet, mud-encrusted material.

"Kathryn, no. You do not want to do that. I'm supposed to protect you. My job is—"

"Jason, yes." She turned to face him, her mouth tucked up to the hollow at the base of his throat. She nipped at his Adam's apple, then his chin. Moving her full lips to tease the corner of his, her tongue flicking out to taste his bottom lip. "Jason," she murmured huskily against his still closed mouth, "Give me what I need, please." Her fingers went to the buttons of her tattered blouse. She slipped a pearly white button through the opening, then another, and another.

Jason's world paused as he drew in a ragged breath. For three drawn out seconds he saw a sliver of an opening, a chance to walk away and leave both his job and his heart intact. Then she slid the curled edges of the flimsy material apart. One long look at her heated flesh, her dark, rosy nipples pushing against the now see through material of the sensible brassiere, and any hope of retreat dissipated. He was lost and he knew it. Fighting a battle he knew there was no way he could win. Mine.

"What is it you want, then?" he asked hoarsely.

The corner of her mouth rose, and her voice went low and husky. "Go down on me, Jason. Taste what you've been missing. Take what you want. What I want to give you. What I need to grant you."

A flick of his thumb and forefinger removed the barrier of the front-opening clasp. Pushing aside the damp material, letting the bra fall to her supple sides, he bent his head to the softness of her breast, taking one stiff, straining nipple into his mouth. Her skin was soft against his lips, but the nipple thrust hard against his tongue. Gently, he swirled his tongue around its base, then lightly grazed its edge with his teeth.

Her soft moan sent shivers of need though his body. Jason tightened his hold on the thickness of her waist. He could spend the entire day right there, sucking, eternally sucking with her writhing beneath his hands. Nothing came close to the feel of her generous, soft body. Nothing.

'Taste what you've been missing.' Oh, he'd taste all right. He'd leave her a quivering, panting, satisfied mess–driven to the brink of insanity and coaxed back only by his touch.

The thought made him suck harder, while with his other hand he flicked her other beaded nipple. She moaned, squirming, but he framed her with his legs, pinning her to the door of the stall with his muscular thighs, rendering her helpless to his touch.

He groaned against her breast as his cock strained, throbbing and painful behind the tight fabric stretched across his hips. He paused without pulling away and closed his eyes, forcing his labored breathing to even out, to quiet his overwhelming desire.

She shifted and began to stroke his hair as her involuntary sounds of pleasure spurred him to fondle and suck again.

"Jason. I can't take it. I can't..."

His gripped her tightly, thumbs beneath her breasts and fingers splayed around her sides.

"Oh, but you will take it, won't you?" he

murmured in a gritty, commanding voice he hardly recognized as his own.

Her chest heaved with deep and difficult breaths as he trailed the tips of his fingers down each side of her body, grasped the edges of her slick, wet jeans, and roughly yanked them and her simple cotton undergarment to her ankles in one swift move. His breath hitched at the sight of her dark curls nestled tight to the apex of her thighs as the musky smell of her sex drifted toward him on the breeze.

He grasped her full backside. Then, using his booted foot to anchor the discarded clothing, he lifted her away from the sodden garments, placing her bare feet on a thick hay bale.

"Grab the beam over your head, Kathryn, and do not let go." he ordered, his voice gruff, hard, leaving no doubt he meant every word.

She raised her arms and did as he bid her, looking down over him with her eyes wide, curious, but she said not a word.

Jason grasped her broad hips and pulled her sex toward him, moving his hand to curl into the thatch of hair. He trailed one finger down to the crease and circled it slowly to trace over her folds.

He wouldn't touch her clit just yet–he'd save that work for his tongue. For now, he let his fingers play over the tension he could feel in her blood-engorged sex.

So wet, so slippery and he'd only just begun. He ached to sink himself into her welcoming flesh. Not yet. No, not yet.

He ran his tongue down her belly, stopping just before he reached her pussy. He separated the folds and brought his face against her smooth, wet skin. His goal was seduction and pleasure until he'd coaxed out complete surrender. He wanted to drain her of every last ounce of her strength.

He blew gently against her heat, and she keened. Then, while sinking a slick finger where his cock so longed to be, he flicked the very edge of his wet tongue on the tip of her swollen clit.

Her head shot up and she arched, bucking her hips, and for a split second almost losing her grip on the wide beam above her.

He followed her movements, darting his tongue in warm circles around the tight bud.

She whimpered, howled, and shook as she released all the pent up tension, her desire covering his lips and chin.

As the last of her orgasm retreated in delicious spasms, Jason grasped her generous buttocks, buried his face against her belly and held her tight. A frightening truth lurked in the corner of his mind. What the hell was he doing? If he gave in to these emotions racing through him he would hurt her, destroy her future. Despite what he wanted in this, what he now knew he couldn't live without, she was innocent and likely didn't have the same long-term goals in mind where he was concerned. He needed to back off, now, before it was too late.

He memorized the sight of her flushed cheeks, her unfocused eyes, her sated and lethargic body, and imprinted the sensual view of her into his mind. God knew he'd use that image so many times in the future. Right now, though, he had to step away, and fast.

Slipping his arms behind her knees, he pulled her down from her perch and cradled her against his chest, regretting what he knew he had to do.

He groaned inwardly as she slid down his hips, brushing against the obvious firmness in his jeans, until her feet met the hay-covered floor.

"Grab your clothes and go have a shower, Kathryn. I have work to do." His gruff, cold tone grated on his nerves but he knew it was the only way. Ignoring the pain and disappointment that flashed across her features, he strode out of the barn, stubbornly refusing his every desire to look back and make sure she was okay.

## CHAPTER NINE

Kathryn had asked Jeanette if she could cook Jason's dinner tonight, and the house manager had thrilled at the idea. Tossing her apron in Kathryn's direction, the woman had smiled and waved as she happily abandoned her post for an evening off, letting the screen door to the mud room slam in her wake.

She'd done her share of exploring the house these past few days since the incident in the barn and needed something else to do to distract her from the hurt. Jason had checked in on her often, but basically avoided her otherwise. Yet, each moment she spent in this house, his house with a masculine design to it, made the ache in her chest grow. The woods were warm or dark, the furniture oversized and rustic with western prints on the couch, rug, and matching wall hangings. She could smell him here, and each whiff made her core burn with a hunger for more. More of him. He wanted her. She'd witnessed the look in his eyes, the way they had darkened to almost black, along with the tenseness in his jaw line. Yes, she believed he saw her and actually wanted her, more than just a quick fling in the barn, but something held him back. Perhaps even something more than just her father or his job.

This hunger, this pure lust and desire, it built in her until the idea cooking for him had come to her, She'd make him feel obligated to sit down and eat with her, figuring it may be her only chance to get him alone and talk to him, or talk him into what she wanted from him. What she wanted after having his mouth on her was to taste him, each and every well-toned muscle, to feel him tense under her touch, but this time to be skin on skin. She'd break him down, but first she had to wow him with her culinary skill, basically gather his attention to her in another way first. That was the plan. All of those cooking classes she'd taken out of sheer boredom after she'd gotten out of boarding school may just pay off. Who could have guessed how, right? She'd certainly never imagined giving those sayings about the way to a man's heart being through his stomach any validity, but it sure seemed she was about to put its truth to the test.

Since she had all day to kill, she started early in the morning surveying the contents of the kitchen. Jeanette had it well stocked. Using her tablet, she searched for some authentic western recipes. She settled on baby back ribs, rubbing them down with a mix of spices and brown sugar, before she made a red chili honey glaze to pour over them. She also made a sweeter version of barbeque beans, some butternut squash with spinach and onions sautéed to put on top, along with green chili cornbread. The kitchen, again dark wood cabinets with granite countertops and all stainless steel appliances, made her feel enveloped in his masculinity as the sweet and spicy aromas of her cooking started to fill the space.

She took one break about midday to go out and visit the puppies, but whether coincidence or not, Jason had exited the barn when she arrived. So, it wasn't until he came in to check on her later that the smells from the kitchen encouraged him to stop and talk to her.

"You cook?" His sweat-slicked body filled the doorframe, his hand grasping the edge of the door.

"I do."

"How did that come about? I assumed you had gourmet chefs at your house and the boarding school to cook for you your entire life or fancy restaurants to dine in."

"I did." She fought the desire to snark back at his comment. "Cooking was a passion I found quite by accident. After boarding school I needed something to entertain me, something to kill time until Daddy found the perfect marriage for me, or whatever." She gestured toward her curvy figure, her hands shaping the air over her breasts and then her bottom, "You may have noticed I like to eat, so this was just a logical thing to try. I found out I enjoy looking up recipes, giving them my own signature touch. The rest, the chopping, the mixing, it relaxes me."

"You are a woman full of surprises. Actually enjoying my ranch, putting up with the animals and the smells. Saving puppies. And, now cooking? What's next?"

"Well, sit down and eat with me and we can discuss that," she offered, looking over her shoulder at him with what she hoped was some subtlety, continually stirring something on the stove that didn't actually need stirring anymore.

"I don't know if that's a good idea. I mean, I do want to taste what I smell, and I'm so hungry I could eat a horse even if it's likely burned to a crisp, but us alone, it just seems too dangerous. You promised not to put yourself in any more danger, remember."

Kathryn felt heat infuse her face at the recollection of what occurred a few days ago in the barn. The promises she made to him were not quite the same as the ones she'd made to herself, though. She pressed on, ignoring his cutting remarks about her cooking, determined to win this round. "Don't be ridiculous. I made all of this food. The least you could do is sit down and eat it. Unless, of course, you want this all to go to waste or you think my cooking may poison you. You pick the dinner topic."

"It's not your cooking I worry about affecting my health," he grumbled under his breath and turned with an exaggerated sigh to go back into the mud room to wash up and remove his dusty boots.

The food had apparently been a huge success, to her relief. He'd gobbled down two helpings of the ribs, a giant portion of the baked beans, raved over her skill with the butternut squash, and wiped up his plate with three large slices of the green chili cornbread. His genuine surprise and appreciation over her ability to prepare such a good meal pleased her. She finally felt like she'd done something right when he sat back in his chair, rubbing his overfilled stomach, clearly sated.

The conversation during dinner had been strained at first, but the more she'd encouraged him to talk about himself, his life up until that point, how he'd come to own the ranch, all the work he'd done on it with his own two hands to make his dream a reality, the more he had relaxed into the conversation.

***

Kathryn literally beamed as Jason stood beside the oven and begrudgingly complimented her over her apple pie. Against his better judgment he'd had to tell her straight up how good the meal had been, and to top it all off she'd chosen to make his absolute favorite pie and added her own special touch to the delicious dessert.

She'd insisted it was such a simple recipe there was truly no way she could have screwed it up even if she'd never taken the cookery classes. Just a few ripe apples, some strong, freshly grated cinnamon–which she claimed to love the smell of, and he'd thoroughly agreed since it was a scent he associated with her entirely–a cup of flour, a dash of salt, and a bit of oil. She'd said she thought her crust turned out more thick and heavy than light and flaky, but Jason sure didn't seem to think so, and didn't mind one bit as he licked the crumbs off his fork from his second piece. The woman could cook. Of that he'd little doubt, now. She was so different here on the ranch, and the combination was getting to him again despite his best intentions to stay clear of her until her time here was up and she could safely return home. In fact, the very idea of her possibly leaving soon sent a shock of electricity to his gut, leaving a very unexpected ache remaining.

"Jason," she said softly, "I want you to make love to me." She ran her hand along his tense and bulging bicep. "Let go of whatever is holding you from me. Show me the real you. Teach me more than just what you do for a living. Teach me what you like in the bedroom. I need to know."

"Kathryn, you don't know what you're asking for."

"Yes, I think I do, Jason. Please."

She peered up at him through thick lashes, eyes shining with unshed tears and want plain on her face. The innocence of this woman had been his undoing, and now her pleading was driving him to the other side of sanity. He needed to make her his, in all ways. No more pushing her away after a quick roll in the hay. Time to show her who he truly was, consequences be damned. Mine. The word ricocheted through his brain and into his heart. Just as she had interfered with his good intentions, now she had gone and changed his plans for the future.

"Damn it, woman!" He let a loud groan escape from his lips.

Without warning, Jason spun her around and pushed her against the edge of the counter, bending her face down so her cheek rested on the cold marble top, her wrists clasped tightly in his thick, calloused grip.

Panting, he flipped up the back of her blue sundress around her waist, and ripped off her sensible, white, lace-trimmed panties.

"Kathryn, you need to be sure. I've held back as long as I can. Men have needs, darlin', and you've pushed me to my limits far too often for me to turn back once I get started here. I won't be able to stop this time. You do know what you're in for with a man like me, right? Tell me you truly get it because the last thing I want to do is hurt you." He ran his hand over her fleshy behind, marveling at the creamy softness of her skin. Imagining how it would feel to sink his cock deep between her cheeks and into her moist heat.

"I understand, Jason. I do, really do. I want this, you, more than you could ever know. You don't scare me."

Jason hissed and sucked in a breath. He leaned over her back, running his hand down between her legs, curling his fingers into her wet crevice. Damn, she was so wet, so ready she could take him twice and not run dry.

Releasing the buttons on his jeans, he pulled his now solid shaft from within the confines of the restrictive material. With a single thrust, he roughly pressed his length deep into her heated core. She was so damn warm and tight. It was all he could do not to come at that very moment.

"Jason, please" she moaned, pushing back against him, encouraging him to take her.

Grabbing the back of her neck and holding her down with his other hand on her back he slammed his hard cock into her. Not even caring as much now if he hurt her a little, she had asked for this, he was only human. A man could only take so much!

"You want my cock, young lady, well now you are going to get it. Time to live dangerously," Jason growled in her ear, as he continued his assault on her throbbing sex. Over and over he pulled his cock from her heat, slamming back in hard every time. She had driven him nuts with her playing, whether she knew it or not, and now it was his turn.

"Do you like that, Kathryn?" he demanded of

her, squeezing her neck a little when she did not answer him. "Is this what you've been after?"

"Yes..." She moaned, panting.

He suddenly pulled out of her, a hiss escaping between his teeth, his cock throbbing, dripping their combined juices from the tip. If he wasn't careful he was going to finish this before they'd even started.

Looking back at him, watching him as he attempted to contain himself, she emitted a long, low, grumbling chuckle. "Am I too much for you Jason?"

His anger at himself for giving in to her, not holding back when he knew he should never have allowed it to go this far, now turned into a sexual need to have her, to own her. He was raging with the feeling of wanting to fuck her so hard she would beg for more, or maybe beg him to stop. Jason was absolutely beyond reality now. He was burning with need, intoxicated by her scent on him, around him, all vanilla and cinnamon saturating the very air he breathed. Beyond all rational thought anymore, Jason only knew he needed to have more of her. He was running on pure male animal lust now, and it was damned dangerous.

Her chuckle seemed only to add to his already heightened mood, as he looked over her body, bent over the counter, legs spread wide and that ass, her perfect, pliable, voluptuous ass. He was almost drooling at the thoughts going through his mind. Even he was surprised at how much he wanted her...how he wanted her.

"I mean, sir," she drawled with something resembling an evil grin crossing her features. She knew she had him. Damn the woman. She'd hit his sweet spot dead on.

Feeling a heat come over him that had nothing to do with the temperature outside, Jason began to sweat with uncontrollable urge. The effort to restrain himself almost killed him.

He smacked her ass, hard, waiting with baited breath to see if she would complain, if she would struggle at the turn of his dominance this time and change her mind. He needed to know if she realized the difference between the spanking in the barn, the chastisement of her childish, unruly behavior, and the sexual need he now attempted to fill for them both. He had to know if he'd misjudged her even the slightest bit, though her calling him sir left very little doubt.

She didn't move a muscle. Much to his amazement, she actually moaned in pleasure. Watching her perfect dimpled butt cheek turn a slight shade of pink almost proved to be his undoing. He smacked her again, a little harder this time, and she swayed back and forth absorbing the pain in her generous behind, pushing her ass back out for more.

"Sir, yes. Please, sir, I need..." Kathryn panted and pressed back against his hand, searching.

Sliding his calloused fingers over the blossoming redness of his handprint on her bottom, he sucked in a breath. He loved the way the outline formed on her ass, almost glowed against her soft, pale skin. "You are going to be the death of me, I swear it."

He leaned down to nip at the back of her neck, his five o'clock shadow chafing against her skin and leaving rosy streaks in the wake of his mouth as he moved over to nibble her shoulder. "In good time, baby. Be patient just a little longer. I won't be able to hold off very long this first time."

Sliding his hand between her thick thighs, he cupped her pussy and feeling the wetness of her, how excited she was, groaned deep in his chest as he entered her with two of his fingers. He began massaging her clit with his thumb as his fingers sought out, curled upward, and found her g-spot.

Moaning and moving against his hand, she pushed back against him. "Jason, please. I need..." she begged him, turning her head to look back at him from under thick lashes, her eyes shining with unspent tears from the sting of the spanking.

He knew she was enjoying herself, her pussy was literally soaking his hand. She was ready for him.

Grabbing his hard cock as he moved his other hand to rest on her thick hip, he lined his hardness up with her center and pushed deep.

\*\*\*

Spreading her thighs with a light kick to each calf, Jason prodded roughly at her entrance, and then letting out a low growl, he slammed forward in a rush, filling her, stretching her. Kathryn cried out at the welcome intrusion, her climax already building, her legs becoming shaky and weak.

She moaned as his fingers dug into her hips, his hands lifting her up and back to meet each deep plunge. He rocked his hips, stroking her pleasure higher. She keened as he passed over the same spot again and again, causing her insides to clamp around him as she reached the edge.

Jason thrust into her, pain and pleasure erupting simultaneously, stealing her breath and carrying her away to ride in ecstasy. She screamed as he forced her through one orgasm after another, pistoning in and out faster and faster, bringing her to completion long after she was sure she couldn't take anymore.

He grunted, dropping down over her back to claim her lips as he emptied himself into her core. Breathing heavily, he pulled his still hard shaft from between her thighs, bending to scoop her up in his arms and cradle her against his chest.

Kathryn snuggled into the crook of his neck, gazing adoringly up at him, eyelids heavy, panting heavily.

He slipped inside the master bedroom and tenderly placed her against the pillows on the large, dark wood, four-poster bed. For a second, she was fearful he would walk out the way he had in the barn, but he drew off his jeans and boxers, pulled his t-shirt over his head, and slid onto the bed next to her, claiming her mouth once again. She knew in that instant she'd never want to leave him, leave this ranch, and could only pray Jason felt the same.

## Chapter Ten

Kathryn woke to the sound of rushing water mixed with the low rumbling tone of Jason's voice. He spoke too quietly for her to hear what he said, but she had a gut feeling she knew who was on the other end of the line. She had no intention of making it easy on anyone.

Slipping into the adjoining bathroom, she spied Jason's burner phone on the counter by the sink, and Jason within the confines of the clear shower doors as steamy water and frothy bubbles sluiced over his tanned skin. Damn. She felt a rush of moisture to her core at the sight of him in all his glory, bicep and pectoral muscles flexing as he ran his fingers through his dark, saturated hair, rinsing it free of the clinging shampoo.

The scent of a woodsy cedar in the moist air of the room told her he'd already used the delicious smelling body wash and was likely just about finished his morning routine.

Kathryn grinned as she yanked open the door to the cubicle and stepped inside. Time to change his morning routine a little.

"Well, howdy, darlin'." Jason drawled, flashing his pearly whites as she slipped in the stall. "I trust you slept well?"

"Oh, I think I slept just fine, Jason. In fact, I feel better than I have in my entire life thanks to you."

"Happy to be of service, ma'am," he teased.

Kathryn traced the smooth, rippled strength of his stomach and the gentle rise and fall of his expansive chest. She ran the edges of her nails down between his ribs, watching in fascination as his cock jerked in response to her touch. Stroking her perfectly manicured fingernails over the ripples in his abdomen, she smirked as he flinched and partially twisted away from the tormenting digits. "Who was on the phone?"

"What?"

"The phone. I heard you speaking to someone just before I came in here." She dug her nails into the tight muscles at his hips when he hesitated.

"Oh, yeah. That." He chuckled. "I called Pete to check in. They caught your stalker. Turns out the new guy, Brian, was in on a deal to get to your Daddy through you and was feeding the stalker guy information about your whereabouts up until the time I decided to bring you here. Something about a big pay off if they could convince the Senator to back down and look the other way in this legislative vote or something. Pete says your Daddy wants you home, today." Jason frowned, his eyes clouding over as he said the last part.

His simple facial expression made her heart soar. He truly didn't want her to go home any more than she wanted to leave, and for the first time in her life she was actually happy, wanted, accepted.

"And if I don't quite feel like going home yet, sir?" She pressed herself against him and opened her mouth over his throat, licking and nibbling over his warm, wet flesh.

Jason's eyes lit up at her words. "Well then, baby doll, I guess I'm going to have to get used to your horrible culinary skills and chasing away all the evil little animals that are out to bite you or trip you up in mud puddles."

Kathryn's laugh ended in a squeal as he grabbed her wrists from where she'd just stroked a sharp nail over his swollen manhood. He forced them over her head, clasping both tight in one meaty palm as he pressed her against the wall of the shower.

Her back hit the cool wall and she gasped, "Jason, not now, not—"

His lips covered hers and his tongue darted in, stealing any further protests.

He reached between them and slipped his hand between her thighs, fingers plunging into her wet heat and she groaned at the intrusion. She was wet. She was ready.

She raked her fingers into his slick hair and bit his bottom lip. Aroused like this, her hunger was an untamed beast that craved all the wild passion he could give. Foreplay and sugary words be damned. She needed to be fucked hard, now.

"Sir, can you...can we disperse with the preliminaries, please?" she begged. "I need you inside me, sir, please."

Jason growled and spun her to face the wall.

Kathryn whimpered and spread her thighs, welcoming his forcefulness. She needed this. She needed him to push her to the edge of sanity like he'd done many times last night. His dominance, the control he exerted in the bedroom, was her newest addiction, and she wondered if she could ever really have enough.

He grabbed her hips and yanked her back against his groin, shoving the thick head of his dick to press against her opening. Her slickness had his cock gliding back and forth between her folds, tormenting her with every brush of the head over her engorged nub. She felt his knuckles brush against her ass as he grabbed himself and guided his thickness inside her entrance. As wet as she was, he could've filled her with one smooth thrust. Instead, he stretched her with shallow strokes, causing her core to clench, desperate to have him all the way inside.

Bracing both hands on the wall she pushed back against him, letting out a silent scream as he continued to thrust in and out, speeding up until the slaps of his pelvis hitting her ass became the only noise that filled the room over the sound of rushing water.

Heat billowed up and out as the first climax tore through her. Another built up before she could recover. The pleasure overwhelmed her and she screamed, "Jason, oh my god, yes. Please, don't...stop...sir."

She made a keening sound, holding herself up with one hand and reaching back with the other to latch onto his hip. He slammed in and brushed her hand away.

His hand fisted in her hair, forcing her to stay

in place. She felt his heat against her back as his mouth covered her shoulder, nipping hard at the sensitized skin. "Behave, woman," he growled. "We do this on my terms, my way. Demanding anything from me will only gain you more punishment."

"Yes, sir," she panted out.

Releasing her hair, he slid his hand down her back and brought it to rest on her generous backside, his thumb slipping between her ass cheeks to press lightly against the sensitive pucker.

"I want to take you here, Kathryn," he traced the outer edge of the tight muscle. "And when you're ready, when I have made you ready to accept my cock in your sweet ass, you will know what pleasure really is."

Kathryn groaned deep in her throat at the mental image he presented along with the increased pressure of Jason's thumb working its way inside her tightness. The idea of taking him in her rear entrance made her heart thud and sent a thrill racing to her core. She couldn't help the soft whimper that escaped her lips as heat gathered low in her belly.

***

Jason sucked in a breath as his thumb breached her tight entrance, the tightening of her vaginal muscles clamping down on his cock deep within her channel.

He'd been hesitant at first, waiting, trying to give her time to get used to the idea of his thumb penetrating her tight ass. Pushing his digit into her little by little, each time pulling back out. He continued to plunge his cock hard against her sweet spot with each thrust. She was so tight; the head of his cock was almost bursting. The deeper he pressed into her taut ring of muscle, the more she relaxed, accepting the intrusion. He stroked the inside of her hole, massaging the thick ring until his thumb slid in and out freely and her moaning had increased in pitch to the point it drove him insane.

She gasped, moaning as he slid his thumb back out and replaced it with two, thick fingers, stretching her gently until she accepted the invasive digits. He moved his hand faster now, alternating with each plunge of his dick into her heated channel as Kathryn panted heavily, pressing back against the pressure in her rear.

He finger fucked her back channel gently at first, but with increasing speed. Both of them were breathing very heavily, sweating, moaning with pleasure and unspent need.

"Jason!" Kathryn screamed as she came, her body shuddering, muscles stiffening as she arched her back, her core clutching around his shaft.

Hearing her call his name sent him flying over the edge into oblivion. He slammed forward once more, his body stiffening as he released his seed deep inside her. Jason continued to gently pump his fingers into her ass, drawing her orgasm out until her trembling and contractions subsided.

He slipped his fingers from the throbbing channel, and gathered her into his arms, pulling her against his chest and nibbling at her arched neck.

He had never, in his entire life, ever felt such intense pleasure and happiness in anything, anyone, like he did at this moment. Kathryn was a natural submissive and he couldn't be more interested in teaching her how to properly behave. Mine.

THE END

## About the Authors

Ms. Gina Kincade has been penning sensual stories since she was seventeen years old.

She writes everything from contemporary mainstream romance, to high heat M/F, M/M, Ménage, BDSM, and fetish. Her evil little vampires and were-creatures will rip out your heart without thinking twice and then engage in steamy, explicit sex scenes.

A busy mom to three children, Gina lives in her wild household of two rambunctious dogs, a devoted, loving cat who believes herself to be royalty, and twelve crazy little chickens. She loves healthy home cooking, gardening, warm beaches, fast cars, and horseback riding.

Ms. Kincade's life is full, time is never on her side, and she wouldn't change a moment of it!

Connect with on Gina on Facebook or sign up for her Newsletter Mailing List

EVER SINCE SHE WAS YOUNG, KIKI HOWELL has loved to listen to a well-woven tale with real characters, inspired plots, and delightful resolutions. Kiki could spend hours lost in a book, and soon she knew that creating lives, loves, and losses with just words had to be the greatest thing that she could do.

Kiki has had over fifty stories published with three novels hitting Amazon Bestsellers lists in categories like Paranormal, Suspense, Occult Horror and Witch & Wizard Thrillers. She's won awards like being chosen as an Ohioana Book Festival author along with having several shorts win writing contests.

Connect with Kiki on Facebook or sign up for her Newsletter Mailing List

# WHERE TO FIND MORE

Find more of Kiki Howell and Gina Kincade's combined and individual works on their websites, blogs, or at all reputable online distributors

KIKI HOWELL

http://www.kikihowell.com/

http://anauthorsmusings.blogspot.com/

GINA KINCADE

http://themistressjournals.blogspot.com/

http://ginakincade.blogspot.com/

COMBINED WORKS

www://kikiandgina.com

*A PREVIEW FROM KIKI AND GINA'S NEXT BOOK...*

# WHEN THE SNOW FLIES

The late fall night threatened a first snowfall. According to the weatherman only a few flurries would fly, but Anna had come out to the labyrinth to walk anyway. Seeing a snow globe world under the nearly full moon would be stunning, if it did happen, so she'd put an imaginary check on the worth freezing my butt off column and jumped in her car. That wouldn't even be out of character for her, as she didn't think straight, or even rationally about life most days. A forced numb feeling guided her most of the time as she struggled to face the realities of her loss and fake moving on for her own benefit. As much as she could manage, she stayed shut away from the real world as humanly possible and disengaged from the majority of her still raw emotions. New York City enabled her to be beyond a wallflower, letting her fade into the rush of life all too easy, no more significant than a speck in the pavement of life.

Anna pried her fingers away from the long sweater jacket she clutched around her to tie an extra knot in her thick scarf at the back of her neck, keeping it out of her way. She had little patience for clothes these days. Once a fashion diva attending college to be a clothing designer, clothes now served her as only cover or warmth with no regard for style. Comfort, camouflage, and cotton, had become the prime constructs in her 'who cares about chic' choices. Her choice tonight—an oversized, calf-length, brown-cabled sweater—had belonged to her mother. The scarf—a thick cable knit, multi-shade with greys and blues and maroons—had been her father's. A T-shirt, some alternative band her sister, Chelsie, had been into, remained hidden underneath the mess. She'd stay as close to warm as she could come, thanks to a set of long underwear leftover from an ski trip that seemed part of someone else's life. Memories she only borrowed, now, but didn't identify with.

So, in reality, she'd become somewhat of a walking shrine to those she missed so severely she often couldn't breathe, the ailment only compounded by the fact the clothing from necessary washes had lost each person's scent. The tragedy of this could not be understated. Yet, she tortured herself, needing to wear what caused her grief. Such had become her semi-lucid existence, run by a faltering psyche as she stumbled through a life of only what she absolutely had to.

Her memory would terrorize her at times. In a bittersweet way, turning the scent of baked goods into the same fragrance as the vanilla cream scent of mother's skin. Her senses were traitors, doing all they could to jab razor sharp sticks at her heart. A heart that seemed to only faintly beat most days. Sometimes, a laugh caught on the wind got through the clatter of the city, making her turn, expecting to see her sister. Other times, the brush of a hand against hers as she made her way along a busy street made her feel like a little girl again. The one her father had insisted on holding hands with when they were out. Only her taste buds remained true, never letting a single thing she ate taste as good as her mother had made it.

She'd long ago given up, run away from the cheap clinic psychologist who told her she wasn't healing, moving on as she should, having given her some bizarre timeline based on some asinine equation of years and loss. The analogy of using a spoon to dig her way through a mountain, or choosing to do the work required to move up one side and down over the other, had only served to enrage her. She'd canceled the next appointment, and never returned to that dreaded chair of despair where her hardships were not allowed to be swept under a rug of new age promises she vaguely sought after to ensure she didn't completely lose her mind to the grief.

The trees, the moon, the small hope of meditation and walking a labyrinth, were all she needed tonight to occupy her overactive mind that stomped on her barely beating heart. A healthy escape, she could claim, at least, save for the danger of possibly getting taken and killed. Still, out here alone in the middle of the night in a New York state park, illegally, after hours, her damaged brain regarded the opportunity as perseverance, endurance, in what amounted to her life.

She sucked a deep breath in through her nose, as she'd read to do, letting it fill her lungs, or what amounted to two hot air balloons ready to deflate and plummet to the solid ground. She attempted to imagine the air as a bright light, filling her, cleansing her chakras. Her whole pagan, new age obsession—a plethora of eclectic beliefs—served as her therapy. Her frail, half-hearted attempt at it anyway. The renegade treatments had yet to work, but her passion for the preoccupation had become a saving grace alone, a delusional neurosis to override all the others. Most nights it served as something to do on her laptop for hours on end. New things to try to pass the time, attempting not to focus on anything else especially not the nightmares that plagued her, sleeping or awake. She'd deemed herself healed, drunk on things like studying elemental representations, getting lost in meditations, and journeying to find her Shadow Self.

Tonight, unable to escape the year old memories as if they'd just occurred, the frequent butterfly visitors to her stomach did a dance of agitation to an unsteady beat. Jittery, like an addict coming down from a sugar high, she'd gone simple in her practice, given what, in her brain-fogged state, she could discern and devise. Walking in a labyrinth with the rustle of the winter wind making the bare limbs of the trees scratch, had been preferable to pacing her already worn-beyond-recognition carpet to the beat of the neighbors having yet another romantic dispute.

So, out here, poised on numb feet, she held tightly to her desperate cause emotionally. While, in reality, in one hand she had a death grip on a polished piece of black onyx, a cleansing stone believed to trap and then ground any negative energy. The damn thing, no bigger than a golf ball, couldn't possibly be big enough to handle hers. Still, it remained one of two lifelines, aiding her fragile grip on moving forward. In her other palm, she used her fingers to roll a hunk of snow quartz meant to seal inner wounds. She persisted, the increasing chill of the rock burning her already cold digits, reminding her she indeed, unfortunately, remained alive. The thought posed as a double-edged sword in her mind.

Sadly, she needed both rocks and then some; more than her pockets could carry. This week had marked an anniversary of the tragic car accident that had robbed her of her family: mother, father, and one beloved younger sister. She'd been the sole survivor, left with scars inside and out, with each date on the calendar from birthdays, to anniversaries, to holidays bringing unbearable reminders in the form of memories she wanted to hide from as much as she cherished them.

On the outside, pale skin bore faint—yet to her, disturbing—designs on her face, cut by fragments of glass. She avoided mirrors as much as she could, but it seemed the whole world made them for her out of things like polished cars and clean windows. A jagged scar the shape of a crescent moon ran from her temple to her ear. To her eyes only, she'd been told, the healed skin tugged, making the corner of her eye wrinkle and curve up slightly on one side. Didn't really matter how discernable it was to others, the reminder to her remained real. From there, the scars trailed through her eyebrows and then down over her cheek. Sometimes, when she caught a brief glimpse at herself in life's many reflective surfaces, the series of scars there resembled a game of hangman.

The remaining scars covered her arms, almost

shredded from shards of glass. Beyond that, a surgical scar marred her abdomen, thicker, redder. While she tried to avoid looking at it, during times of high stress, home alone, she found herself often fingering it, making the overly sensitive skin sing with light, pain-spiked sensations inciting her lungs to shudder and her eyes to tear.

On the inside, with temperamental, overwrought affections, she imagined her spirit to be a tattered sheet blowing in a violent storm set to the unsteady thundering of her heart. Orphaned, even if at twenty, still wasn't an easy road, not with murmurings of post-traumatic stress disorder as the order of the day. She had organs inside that had been injured and fixed, bled and been stitched, and the symbolism of that in reference to the way she felt so damaged could not be understated.

Just a few weeks after the torturous funeral obligations had ended, the events of which she'd missed due to healing herself, when well-meaning people, lots of friends of the family, finally began to give her some time alone, she'd packed up her previous life. Still dealing with stitches and bandages, she'd taken only what she assumed in her grief she would want some day. She'd basically filled the trunk of her car and abandoned her childhood home for a destination undeclared. She'd fled from her small hometown full of wonderful memories that abused her mind with each awkward, excruciating breath she was forced to take.

She'd landed in New York, at the time loving the way the crowds hid her, allowing her to disengage. Big city living had that absurd irony of being able to be alone easily within large crowds of people. The boxes she'd packed remained unopened in her tiny apartment, serving as the only table in the dingy place. Covered by a towel, they housed her laptop along with the clutter of living from junk mail to half-drunk mugs of coffee. Within a month of being there, she'd failed to return to college when the new semester began, hadn't even thought to sell the house, and secured a sad excuse for a part time job to pay for necessities. All she actually needed was four walls and a roof, some meager amounts of food, and a library card.

Lately, she passed many a sleepless night at this labyrinth out in the middle of nowhere. She found the hour drive just as cathartic. Being out on the open back roads with few cars, she could fly away from it all: her life, her loner existence, along with the horrid nightmares whether asleep or awake. Alternately, she had a hard time driving at all during the day, especially in traffic, and never on sort of interstate like where the accident had occurred. She walked to work, to the grocery store, to everything from her dinky apartment.

Wandering near traffic often torture enough, she flinched at the squeal of brakes and the crunch of fender-benders—all too common predicaments. It all caused flashbacks. So she used her mother's car only for trips like these: late night and backwoods. Without her need to get away, to lose herself in a dark mess of trees, she'd probably never have gotten in a vehicle again. A necessary evil.

Hardly a soul outside of work knew her name. Maybe her face from the stores she frequented. She figured most couldn't forget the scared beauty, a term she'd overheard a whispered in her own home few times in the days after she'd gotten out of the hospital. The tense lines of people's mouths and big puppy dog eyes she received most of the time confirmed reactions. Although, no one asked her name, or even made small talk here. Even though she did little to groom, her gift of thick, blond waves of hair framed her thin face hosting ocean blue eyes.

She'd been deemed a beauty before, and she figured now people only saw her scars and thought 'what a tragedy.' If they only knew. Her lost physical appearance, simple collateral damage mattering little in the scheme of it all. She pitied those who didn't know that, even as she mourned how she'd learned the lesson. Her anger remained a viable entity pulsing inside of her, keeping her sane, holding the ache of the sorrow at bay.

A harsh breeze with bitter cold undertones picked up, tossing her blonde waves in its grip. Strands, that should have tickled, scratched against her already nearly frozen face. The overly sensitive scar tissue gave off the odd sensation of pinpricks before going numb. The rustle of the fall tree branches screeched, sending an eerie tingle snaking down her spine. With her coat and scarf on, facing the wind, her back had been about the only part of her still warm, and yet now she thought invisible cold fingers tapped from her neck to her waist.

Ghosts came to mind. Real ones, maybe. As she existed haunted by the ones in her mind on a daily basis, oddly this idea didn't seem so far off, and brought a sense of frivolous, insane comfort. Not physical, but mental apparitions. The images of her family, their final moments, like wisps of smoke that groaned, existed in her mind—vivid, real. Something beyond any horror movie she'd ever seen. To have them, any semblance of them, in real life, even if incorporeal beings, would have to be better than what she possessed of them now. Things. Memories. Shaking the chill off until pain shot through her head temple to temple, she closed her eyes tight so that when she opened them, dots, like dirty snow, moved over where she looked down at her shoes.

Old, worn boots, nothing practical for walking, stood just at the edge, the line on the ground where grass gave way to soil, that began the circular path of the labyrinth. A tear slipped from her blinking eye and nearly froze on her face. She took it all in stride. This weather made her feel alive while she remained dead inside. A phantom on this earth herself, she floated through, did the bare minimum to survive unless you called stocking shelves a few nights a week at a local superstore and living on ramen noodles and weak coffee a life. Not that she would have needed the money if she'd been able to sell the house. The thought crossed her mind often, only to be crossed out again. She couldn't, not yet, just like she couldn't open the few boxes of stuff she'd packed from it. The clothes of theirs, a few of their favorites that she'd put in her suitcase, would remain, for now, her only ties. Those shreds of fabric made her feel attached to them still, at least as much as she could bear.

A few more deep breaths later, she shivered violently, but began her trek around the labyrinth. She stumbled a few times over the stones that edged the pathway when patches of clouds blocked out the moon's light. Looking up, she expected to just see a glimmer of white brilliance fighting to shine through the delicate filaments, which had become infused with dark grey matter. Instead, a shadow flew over her. One too large to be anything her mind could figure out.

She hadn't realized that she'd fallen to a crouch until her body swayed as she looked up, trying to get a better look at what had to be a plane or something descending to the earth. Strangely, she hadn't heard a sound. In fact, the eerie silence unnerved her further, leaving her trembling fingers against the frigid dirt to be her only source of support. Falling to her butt as she followed the tremendous mass, she made out a body too rounded for a plane, with wings too animal-like to be inanimate. In a split second, a scream lodged in her throat as the wing things flapped, rustling the tree branches with sudden gusts of air. A long tail seemed to follow behind, swinging to one side as it glided effortlessly around to come back her way, losing altitude as it moved.

She'd stayed in that odd position, seated on the ground, body curled up, with one arm back holding her up as the other one covered her face while the ground shook beneath her when the beast landed maybe ten feet away. With her heart pounding so hard she could hear the erratic beat of the damned thing in her head, she blinked several times as the image before her registered to fantastical proportions. The fact that Anna saw something out of a storybook or a fairy tale made the only sense her perceptions could come up with, and that unnerved her. So much so, she was wound her up like a clock about to explode, spewing gears and gadgets all over the place. The analogy for her head being about to explode based on an image from an old cartoon she'd watched as a child gave her pause. A moment of lunacy that served as a much needed reprieve since reality didn't make any sense at all.

Coping mechanisms. She'd heard a lot about them in therapy. In fact, she'd basically left the practice since she hadn't been ready to give them up. Snippets of songs would come into her head now, memories from childhood of dancing like a loon in the kitchen with her mother when holidays provided long days of baking. These created a preoccupation with remembering every word of the tune, looking up the video, studying the career of the singer, all in an attempt to calm the sudden onslaught of tears. To numb the painful ache in her chest.

At times, she raged at her body. Her heart had the audacity to feel like it had stopped beating if even for a second. Her lungs deflated, ceased to do their job. All of these sensations served as a tease when she had to remain in this life, too squeamish, too much a coward, to end her own though she'd failed their suicide test more than a few times. The desire to find peace in the afterlife with her lost family repeatedly trampled by a lesson on suicide and sin her mother had once taught her. Though as far as beliefs went, anything to do with faith and religion, she didn't even know what or if she believed anymore. The closest thing she'd gotten to prayer was the screaming in her head. The raging at some invisible entity around her so called life.

This confusion continued, rattling her to her core, as she and this thing, whatever the hell it was—and hell-born it could be given its monstrous size and shape—stared at her. Metal-colored eyes glistened in the faint, cloud-covered moonlight. The size of footballs, they blinked in a never-ending gaze that mesmerized her. The world seemed to spin as millions of overacting nerve cells tensed her muscles to run. Yet, move she didn't for some strange fear of being swallowed up whole or burnt to a crisp like in those stories of dragons. Sadly, as her eyes focused, the more this thing as tall as a house resembled just such a mythic creature. If prey moved it got eaten seemed the fundamental law guiding her decision to remain a statue.

Her brain screamed things like the fact that dragons didn't exist. Simultaneously, thoughts swirled to reconcile the sight before her, to dig out of her mind a category of being that would explain away rationally this creature whose hot breath bathed her entire body, small puffs of smoke emanating from its long, regal nose. Crystalline white scales gleamed in the reappearance of the moonlight, as the clouds parted to grant her a better look. The light made the creature the color of fresh fallen snow. This had not been what the meteorologist had predicted would fly tonight though.

The beauty of the beast with scales that sparkled like frozen snowflakes, remained unrivaled in any picture she'd ever seen of a dragon. Painted ones of course, as you couldn't take a photograph of something that didn't exist. So, laying her cards on it being a hallucination sounded her best bet right now. Apparently she'd managed to get high on the night air, on the scent of threatening snow.

"You're not real," she mumbled to herself. The massive beast cocked its head to one side like a dog did when you spoke to them. Her sister's dog, a German Shepard named Sheba, had done that when it caught one of the two words it knew like 'food' or 'outside'.

This was no puppy though, not even a full-grown beast of a dog. This animal towered over her a few stories high. It continued to sit in a sovereign pose though she willed the image away. The moon behind him, or her, or it, now glimmered through the wings, making them look angelic despite the absence of feathers and the tattered edges.

"This isn't happening," she said aloud, forcefully, the effort scraping her dry throat. "I'm having a break down brought on by depression, anxiety, cold...something. Anything. If I could just pass out. If only... Say something," she begged of the animal. "No, on second thought, even if you can, please don't. I might just have a heart attack."

It lowered its head in response, shaking it to

and fro, gently, with grace, yet the ice pick like horns crowning the top of its head gave the gesture a threatening feel.

She backed up, or more like inched along the ground on her ass, hoping the movements indiscernible. Not her luck, though. Instead, her actions seemed to incite the thing.

The brute tensed its body, front legs stiffening, lengthening, chest puffing out further. With a near deafening snort, the mammoth-sized apparition opened its mouth a little and she actually waited for it to speak. This was some sort of hallucination. It had to be. So, she figured why wouldn't it talk, too?

"Go away," she cried out in a low whisper.

The creature stomped all four feet on the ground as if repositioning, which only served to create small seismic tremors under her. She scrambled to her feet to run, the instinct finally kicking in beyond reason to run straight out of the labyrinth to her car in hopes of finding her sanity there. One step, a stumble, and another straighter step later, she heard the whoosh of a back draft, and felt the heat around her. Looking back over her shoulder, she stopped dead in her tracks.

The monster moved its head in a circle, creating flames around her, causing the untended grass surrounding the labyrinth to catch fire instantaneously.

Trapped, panicked, she lost consciousness, her world fading to black as the beast lowered his head toward her.

A SPIN OFF BONUS SHORT STORY

MAJORS CREEK RANCH SERIES

BY GINA KINCADE AND KIKI HOWELL

## BRINGING HIM HOME

"Remove them."

The simple command had Jeanette reacting quickly, instinctively.

She met Sebastian's eyes directly, daringly, watching his features as he gazed longingly at her while she slowly slipped the lace panties over her hips, down her thighs, slipping them from one high-heeled foot at a time. She stood, waiting for his command.

"Come here," he breathed quietly, a single finger cocked in gesture.

Jeanette dropped to the bed, kneeling in front of him, letting out a hushed moan as his fingers touched her hair gently, fleetingly, and began to trail a path from her cheek, over her puckered nipples, down to her moist center. His touch electric, little jolts of pleasure arced up her body wherever he made contact with her skin.

"Suck me."

Jeanette bent over his exposed hips, flicked her moist tongue over her parted her lips, and enveloped him in her mouth, tasting the salty evidence of his excitement. She placed her hand on the root of his shaft and heard him moan softly.

She moved her mouth up and down his cock with unveiled enthusiasm, shyly watching through her lashes as Sebastian tossed back his dark head, arched his back, and groaned low in his throat. She anticipated the moment he would swell within her mouth and she'd know he was close.

She moved her other hand to cup his balls, pulling them down and slowing the pressure building inside, lightly stroking the underside near his ass with her knuckle, thrilling at the long, deep moan that escaped his lips.

Sebastian's gaze traveled to meet hers and she noticed the lust-filled haze within the depths of the chocolate brown orbs. The intensity of his stare made her blush, but still she watched him: waiting. Jeanette bobbed her head faster, moving one hand up and down his length in time with her mouth.

His breathing became more agitated. His eyes began to close, and he brought his hands to the sides of her face.

"Jeanette, enough." He pulled back, withdrew himself from her mouth.

She felt an inexplicable loss all the way to her core. "Sir, I...did I do something wrong?"

"No, Jeanette. Not at all. Tonight is simply going to be a little different is all." Sebastian smiled down at her, trailed his fingers over her flush-warmed cheek.

Jeanette's heart soared with the knowledge he was pleased with her. Curious, though, her thoughts raced through her mind trying to determine what he meant by different. They'd been together this way for months prior to his recent few week absence, ever since he'd started working at Majors Creek, and she couldn't imagine what may have changed between them to make him decide tonight should be any different.

Thrilled when Jason's new guest, Kathryn Caruthers, had decided she wanted to make a meal, thus giving Jeanette a very much appreciated night off, she had taken advantage of the free time to go into town to pick up a few things needed at home. She ran into Sebastian at the Tool & Tack shop along the way. She hadn't even known he'd returned, and despite a twinge of pain making it's way through her heart, she'd approached him as if she'd seen him only yesterday.

When Sebastian realized she'd had an actual entire evening to herself, his eyes lit up in unveiled excitement and he'd invited her for dinner at the local restaurant, a mom and pop run place called The Chandler Inn. She'd happily accepted after not seeing him in the last few weeks.

Unexpectedly, when they'd finished the delicious home-style meal of medium rare steak, baked potatoes, and freshly cut green beans, he'd picked up a key for one of the rooms in the Inn. Lightly grasping her by the hand, he's pulled her out the door and across the parking lot to the small, two-storey hotel.

Jeanette gasped as Sebastian reached down and, cupping her chin, guided her to stand. She wasn't used to this from him. The change in his behavior made her nervous as he pushed her down to recline on her back and pulled her to the very edge of the bed. For a long moment he waited, his breath coming fast and heavy.

Slowly, attentively, he spread her legs apart, kneeling down to kiss her thighs, stroking the edge of his tongue across her skin, his face rapturous as he lowered himself closer to her sex. She could feel his breath trailing across her silky folds, hear him inhaling the sweet smell of her.

He lifted his gaze to Jeanette's face, leaned forward, and without touching it, blew gently on her clit.

She gasped, arching her back at the shock of electricity through her core.

Sebastian moved the tip of his tongue up and down her moist folds tasting her excitement as she bucked her hips in response. Without warning, he drove his tongue inside her, pressing his face hard into her body. Jeanette jolted, letting out a loud moan as he grabbed her by the hips and pulled her body toward him, savagely stabbing her again and again with his tongue.

He withdrew and held his mouth over her clit, waiting, his striking dark caramel-colored gaze watching her face closely, looking for what exactly, she didn't know. A reaction she hadn't offered? Did she screw up and miss something he'd expected of her?

Sebastian had avoided touching her most sensitive part, so when his tongue finally made contact with her aching clit, Jeanette felt herself convulse, arching backward as her channel clamped down on air, her body willing some intrusion to seize itself upon.

Jolts of pleasure shook through her body as he flicked his tongue up and down her clitoris, gently sucking the swollen nub as he softly caressed her inner labia with his fingertips. He enveloped her with his mouth, using his lips, stroking her with his tongue, moaning loudly, his enjoyment of her sex becoming very evident as she felt his voice vibrate against her body. His fingers trailed up and down her slit, feeling her wetness. Carefully, gauging her reaction, he expertly pressed two fingers slowly inside her.

Jeanette felt as if the room had begun to spin. She closed her eyes in an attempt to ward off the virtual rotation but it didn't help. She was suddenly acutely aware of everything. His warm mouth surrounding her sex. His hot breath against her flesh. His soft, heated lips stroking her in time with his tongue.

*His tongue.* She was intensely aware of his tongue: how it felt, how it moved, the texture of it as he swirled it around her clit. His fingers moved faster inside her.

"Come for me." Sebastian's deep, gravelly voice vibrated against her, only adding to her sensitivity.

Jeanette began to feel the familiar tremors building up inside her. She struggled to control the flooding response at her core as her senses reeled.

He stood and moved up between her legs, placing his cock at her swollen, waiting entrance. She felt his manhood pulsing against her. For a few moments he just held it there, twitching, leaking beads of his excitement.

Sebastian groaned deep in his chest and rubbed himself up and down her slit, gently moving the tip across her eager clit. Jeanette felt a shock of intense pleasure, her body opening to him.

He fixed his gaze on her face, then slowly, deliberately, penetrated her until just the head of his cock was inside of her.

Jeanette's muscles contracted and pulsated around him.

He moaned and pulled himself out with the same unhurried pace.

Her body registered the sense of loss immediately, and she moaned in agitation, wanting desperately for him to fill her. "Please," she begged, her eyes imploring him to continue.

He pushed his cock back into her warmth, withdrawing repeatedly, moving inside her inch by inch until he was halfway in, surrounded by her warm engorged flesh. He withdrew his hardness again at the same achingly slow rate.

Sebastian started pumping her faster, still never putting his full length into her. He licked his fingertips and moved them to her clit, stroking it. Waves of pleasure rose from somewhere deep inside Jeanette's being, threatening to engulf her.

"Uh, Sebastian...sir, you feel so good. Please."

He started thrusting into her, faster and deeper. His fingers sliding up and down her clit.

Jeanette felt the sensations rising up inside of her, the tremors within the walls of her sex getting stronger; starting to consume her. His gaze held hers captive: mesmerizing, imploring. She couldn't look away.

"Come for me. Please," Sebastian panted out.

"I...I can't. I want to..." Jeanette bucked against his hips, her back arching.

He pounded into her furiously. His hand at her clit continued to move faster and faster. He pushed himself into her fully, his cock completely surrounded by her twitching, aching flesh.

His face contorted in pain, his eyes grew moist and he leaned forward, moving to cover her body with his. His mouth urgently sought hers, but still he kept his vibrant shadowy russet eyes locked onto hers. His hands were at her hips, pulling her up and into his savage thrusts.

"I love you." He moaned against her lips.

Jeanette felt something at the center of her being tremble and then give way. Her world felt like it suddenly exploded. She couldn't breathe. She couldn't think. He really loved her? Everything she'd been holding back, the feeling of losing him, thinking he didn't care, rushed forth in a flood of raw emotion and pure pleasure.

They came together. Her body convulsing wildly as wave after wave of sexual bliss pulsed through her. Feral screams reverberated in the room. He thrashed against her as he felt her muscles contract around him uncontrollably, electric surges of pleasure shooting out from somewhere in the center of her being.

As her orgasmic spasms died down, she realized the wild screams had been issued from her own throat.

They sprawled side by side, exhausted. Their chests heaved up and down together, breathing in sync. Sebastian wrapped his arms around her, pulling her close. He kissed her swollen lips softly and told her again how much he loved her. His words were soothing in her ear.

Jeanette snuggled into his warmth, lulled by the tone of his voice telling her how much he'd missed her, *them*, the sweet syllables echoing gently in her heart. The last thing she was aware of before drifting off into oblivion was his dark hair falling softly across his coarse cheeks, the steady beating of his heart, and his face pressed against her own.

She fell into a deep sleep with his lips against her neck and the sound of him inhaling the scent of her skin. Finally content.

58433725R00110

Made in the USA
Charleston, SC
10 July 2016